New York was an all-night party of lovers, music, and dreamers. . . .

But for Francine, a sultry young singer, and her lover, Johnny, a temperamental musician, the party ended as the realities of life crept in: a child born of their hasty marriage, Johnny's discontent with his career, the lovers he faked to goad Francine. And then, they both were hoping for the big break. . . .

New York, New York

A bittersweet love story of the years when the past was quickly forgotten and the future stretched magnificently ahead. A novel of two people making it—or not making it—in the elusive dream world of jazz before it was mass-manufactured.

NEW YORK, NEW YORK

by

EARL MAC RAUCH

A KANGAROO BOOK
PUBLISHED BY POCKET BOOKS NEW YORK

Distributed in Canada by PaperJacks Ltd., a Licensee
of the trademarks of Simon & Schuster, a division of
Gulf+Western Corporation.

NEW YORK, NEW YORK

Simon and Schuster edition published 1977

POCKET BOOK edition published May, 1977

This POCKET BOOK edition includes every word contained in
the original, higher-priced edition. It is printed from brand-new
plates made from completly reset, clear, easy-to-read type.
POCKET BOOK editions are published by
POCKET BOOKS,
a division of Simon & Schuster, Inc.,
A GULF+WESTERN COMPANY
Trademarks registered in the United States
and other countries.
In Canada distributed by PaperJacks Ltd.,
330 Steelcase Road, Markham, Ontario.

ISBN: 0-671-80850-8.
Library of Congress Catalog Card Number: 76-55701.
Printed in Canada.

ALL THAT JAZZ

Chapter 1

JOHNNY BOYLE WAS DYING OF SHAME AS HE PUSHED open the heavy door into the world of jazz. This was when he was thirteen. You've all seen the movies, the Dick Powell–June Allyson sort of flick where they're doing somebody's life and the hero is played by a kid actor until he reaches the age of puberty, at which point Dick Powell steps in as though it were a natural process of evolution. One minute an unknown kid and the next minute a star; if you blink twice, you can miss the transition. Yet audiences seem never to complain of the incongruity of Dick Powell playing an unknown kid and vice versa. Maybe they're even amused. These days when everybody seems to know the rules of motion-picture-making, it's understood that the movie tycoons aren't going to stand around waiting for the kid to grow up. But what a great movie it would make if they did just that. Execs might die off, writers, directors, cameramen. Everybody dies except the kid, and he's just getting old. Finally, at the end of his life, they release the movie, and it's so authentic. Maybe one scene took five years to shoot, waiting for the aging process. But then what happens is the kid doesn't make it as a star at any age. He's a broken old man, and his only picture now loses a bundle. The execs who are left turn to each other in the screening room and say, "We should have listened to Father and used Dick Powell."

That's a little exaggerated, but you get the idea. In everybody's life there's a time when the kid actor bows out and the proven box office steps in. It doesn't have to be a big story. It can be a little story. Johnny Boyle wasn't a big story as big stories go. You've probably never even heard of him, but he definitely had a movie in him somewhere. He probably even saw himself in technicolor, knowing Boyle. He probably also thought there wasn't any actor going who could play him up to snuff. That's the kind of fellow he was, cocky and a little aggressive, overbearing, if you know what I mean.

The first scene in the movie is his birth. We get that out of the way quickly. His father, played by Leon Ames, or somebody with a mustache, runs down the street of ramshackle apartment buildings handing out cigars to street venders. It's very picturesque, a lot of immigrant types who speak accented English and maybe don't even understand what Leon Ames is saying. They look at him with puzzled expressions and take the cigars.

"It's a boy! It's a boy!" he shouts and runs on to the next one. PAN BACK TO THE APARTMENT BUILDING where the family lives, and you hear a baby crying. CUT INSIDE, and there's Johnny Boyle, the cutest little baby you ever saw being held by the immigrant woman who delivered him, the midwife. He cries a couple of times, but then he's handed over to his mother, who's smiling, naturally. She takes him, and they both gurgle at each other. That's the first scene of the movie.

"Don't cry, Johnny," his mother says.

The only trouble with that is, Johnny Boyle was born in 1920 and they had hospitals. He was delivered by a doctor, and he never knew his father. Oh, he saw him occasionally, but he never knew the man was his father. He thought he was his aunt's husband, and he was. Uncle Barry. For the sake of family unity, his mother never opened her mouth. Later on, he got a stepfather, but that's another movie.

CUT BACK TO LEON AMES, noticing his son's musical proclivities at an early age. CUT TO MUSIC STORE, CUT TO MUSIC TEACHER, CUT TO JOHNNY'S DISCOVERY

OF JAZZ, as he sneaks into a night spot over on the wrong side of the tracks. He's only thirteen. In two more scenes he'll be Dick Powell.

Johnny Boyle was handsome around the mouth. It was his most pleasing feature, like some guys have merry eyes. His lips were developed to an uncommon degree, as was his bullshit.

"What color's Uranus?" was his favorite line with the girls of London. It was so juvenile, so direct, the sort of thing the English expected of Americans. This was around 1943, and Johnny was never one to disappoint, unless you happened to love him, but that's later in the story, an hour into the movie.

At any rate, the line got him attention. And it set him apart, which was what he craved the most. He had to be different even if it meant making a conscious effort, and that's what he did. He liked being looked on as one of those maniacs who never quite drop over the edge, who hang around and make the rest of us feel lifeless by comparison. It was the big story in him, the star. At heart he was as scared as the rest of us, but up front it didn't show. If he bragged, it meant he privately had his doubts, and below his cool-cucumber front he was nothing but a spoiled brat, a trifle obnoxious about everything that came his way. More than a trifle, if you became close to him. If you call that being a genius, he was a genius. More than likely he was just lonely. He had trouble thinking of himself as a human being among other human beings. They might be human beings, he wasn't sure. But he was sure he was something else.

There were times when, like a little kid, he made a point of announcing what he was about to do even as he was doing it. It was weird. He would be sitting in a chair and he'd say, "I think I'm gonna walk across the room," and he would walk across the room. Or he

8

would be lying in bed and say, "I'm gonna get up now," as if it mattered somehow. "I'm getting up." And he would get up. "I'm gonna get a drink." And he would get a drink, true to his word, making a big production out of it, the point being that he considered what he was doing at any particular minute the most important thing in the world. Newsworthy, if you will. He thought that if he went to the john, it would be a matter of discussion while he was away. By today's standards, he might have been called a megalomaniac, suffering from acute paranoia. In those days he was just called a character, and the war seemed to bring them out of the woodwork. Another example. If he felt good in a place, he would say, "I'm happy here." If he ate something good, it was "I like to eat this." Enough? You get the picture. He had a couple of bearings just a trifle off-center. More than a trifle, if you became close to him.

Still, once you caught him in action, he was something to marvel at. Smooth as silk, a real operator whose wheels you could hear turning like loose change in his pocket. If something caught his eye, he went right after it. He didn't believe in wasting time and he had definite tastes, pro and con. He knew what he wanted when he saw it and went to the heart of it. Life was a watermelon, and he meant to have it all. That he had no idea in general what he wanted out of life except the best parts could be overlooked on these occasions of fleeting brilliance. The guy had technique.

There were dozens of examples, most of them young ladies. He took the line out and dusted it off. "Excuse me, but what color's Uranus?" The lady's jaw would drop a notch, and if she had any self-respect, she would slap him. Even if she didn't have any, she would slap him anyway. It was that too-cute mouth of his.

But through it all he would keep smiling, sizing up her figure while he pointed over to half a dozen Musketeers sitting at a table across the room, all in their Air Corps jackets, all holding pound notes in their sweaty fists, and all of them smiling to the point of being ridiculous, which they were anyway. And it would be up to Johnny Boyle, the unflappable operator, to explain to the young lady: "You see, it's about Uranus. My buddies and me have a little bet riding. I say Uranus is pink, and they say it's purple. Which is it?"

If she could utter a word at all, it was something like "You expect me to tell you!" Question mark. Or, "I beg your pardon," which was the ladylike thing, and walk away. But so few did it, and that was the curious part. Traumatic as one's first encounter with Johnny Boyle might be, something about him persuaded you to stick around. Maybe because you always had the hunch something better was coming up. He'd hit you with something and you kept expecting the topper. Anyway, the ladies hardly ever chose not to play.

"No," you could hear him say, gesturing earnestly with his hand. "You don't understand."

"I certainly don't!"

What a howl that got back at the round table where the Musketeers were hanging on every overheard word, leading one to conclude that the real wager did not concern the color of Uranus in the least.

"You see, everybody knows Mars, the red planet," he would say, perhaps thinking the time right to curl his hand gently under her elbow. "Saturn's got the ruddy rings, Neptune's green with envy, but—" pausing here, for dramatics—"but what color's Uranus? Nobody seems to know that one."

"No, why, not many people do," she would say, stammering and embarrassed now at her own behavior, her own readiness to ascribe obscene motives to a perfectly innocent astronomical question. No wonder if she felt a little ashamed of herself, and such a nice-looking young man, too. Certainly no harm intended. Nothing that you couldn't find in the Encyclopaedia Britannica. She would manage a nervous smile, and a few more words had to follow for protocol's sake. She liked the looks of him in the Air Corps uniform, the bombardier's patch and the burning of Dresden in his eyes. She would apologize, he would apologize. But by then it was all window dressing, and they both knew it. He had her, and he made it look so easy.

"Maybe we oughtta look into this business of Uranus a little further," he would offer. "I know where there's a telescope. It's a nice night tonight."

And the boys at the table sent up a groan, though in reality they loved it. At least one of them was scoring on a regular basis, and money changed hands as Johnny left the place with the lady in tow, having again achieved phenomenal results with his knowledge of the planets. This happened so often that after a while all bets were off, Johnny a victim of his own success, and instead, his buddies tried to steal his line, hoping to discover his secret word by getting into position to eavesdrop. The only trouble with this was, Johnny spotted them coming and made the necessary last-minute adjustments—as if it made any difference to the outcome. He picked up the lady anyway, and the others were still shaking their heads at hearing the oldest line in the book.

"Haven't we met somewhere before?" Johnny asked a blonde.

"On Uranus," she smiled, reaching for her purse.

That was why they couldn't understand. It was all a matter of beat, timing. You either had it or you didn't, and our hero had it in abundance. It must have come from his other love, music. CUT TO LEON AMES AND JOHNNY'S MOTHER, both of them watching as the kindly old music instructor teaches Johnny the workings of the saxophone, beating his pointer on the desk.

"The rhythm, Johnny. Pay attention to the rhythm."

But there was no need. Johnny had the rhythm, and he had a lot more. You can't pin a saxophone on paper, but he could sure take the wraps off it. Ask anybody. He practically slept with the sax when the situation presented itself. He played it on the toilet, and he played it when lights were out. It was good for the soul, he said, and the notes in the lower register soothed his ulcer when he put the bulb of the horn against his stomach. Before the war he had his own big band back in Pittsburgh, where he came from. At least that's what he said. He was always a little sketchy about details, but at the same time you didn't sell him short. He was great on the horn, and if he said he had a band in Pittsburgh before the war, well, it was probably true. But all that was prewar, and ask anybody who came home from the war, prewar was prehistory. He wasn't going back to Pittsburgh anyway, so it was all academic. There was only one town, really, for a guy like Boyle, and at heart he knew it. As soon as the war was behind him, he was headed for New York, a place he thought he'd take by storm, and sooner or later he did. But in the meantime he lived a life he hadn't counted on, like most of the rest of us.

Chapter 2

CUT TO NEW YORK, TIMES SQUARE. NIGHT. IF YOU were there, you've never forgotten it. Even if you weren't there, you probably have the impression you were, because it left quite an impression. It was one of those days and places that become a part of the national consciousness, the common folklore, if you will. You may have seen the photographs, the famous one—the sailor kissing the nurse in the center of Times Square. It was like that. Craziness. V-J Day, the original. NIPS CALL IT QUITS, the papers said, or in more couth words to the same effect. For those of you too young to remember, we were on top of the world, we Americans. Who else was there? What else did you want to be but an American? The world was our mushroom, or something like that. It may seem odd today, but we believed in ourselves. If we had doubts, they were personal ones. America was the greatest.

And you can forget 1900, while you're at it. The twentieth century began in August 1945, with the hairy beast that arrived in Hiroshima. The hairy beast, the black dog, the pink horse—call it any of those things and add your own pet monster or two. We didn't know much about that then. All we knew was that what had gone before could pass as playing around. Now it was the big boys, and until somebody else came along, we were the biggest on the block. The bomb had brought victory, and we weren't going to turn down the winner's roses on the basis of sportsmanship. Maybe we had bought the peace at Filene's basement rate, but there were a lot of people who would argue with you, maybe even get a little irrational. Guys who had lost buddies or a piece of themselves over there, mothers, sisters, sweethearts, kids. Thousands of GI's who had bought the peace, the quick and the dead, and we the living weren't in any mood to apologize. All that would come later, along with the rest of the doubts.

But who said *peace?* This was *peace?* A mauling, brawling mob that looked like millions of stone-eating termites out the window of Johnny's hotel room. Teeming humanity, or inhumanity, as far as the eye could see, swarming like King Kong's fleas at the foundations of famous landmarks, eating away at the cornerstones until the buildings shook. When they filled one street, they turned and spilled over into another. Horns

13

honking, noisemakers, a sea of red, white and blue, cocksuckers who never went to war kissing Gold Star mothers. What the Axis hadn't been able to do in four years, New Yorkers did themselves, with the help of a few out-of-town guests. From Johnny's perch on the eleventh floor, he watched Manhattan get blitzed, then turned his back on them all from a lack of interest.

Buttoning his shirt, he got a load of himself in the mirror and had to feel pleased, all things considered. Not a scratch on him to show for it and in the best health of his life, he'd been going full tilt all day and was beat. The clock said eight, and now he was about to go back, about to try the mob scene downstairs all over again, secure in the confidence that whatever fatigue his muscles knew would vanish as soon as he hit the street. Like everyone else, he looked forward to the best of times, unheard-of prosperity, starting with tonight but by no means ending there. It was the American religion all of a sudden, believing that the worst was past, a belief in the future based on nothing more concrete than a sigh of relief and Yankee know-how. No one knew what it would bring, only that it was to begin immediately by public decree, if not sooner. Perhaps that accounted for the promising and hopeful look on Johnny's face, although with him it was impossible to tell. He could just as easily have been thinking the most morbid thoughts, and they would have shown up in the same sort of smile. But, no, Johnny too was a believer, and a believer above all in the careful art of timing. He fancied this moment his grand entrance, in a manner of speaking. No spiraling staircase or grand hurrahs, but at least the unwanted intrusions were out of the way, and time was again in and counting. Four years of his life, wasted years, hung on a clothes hook in the bathroom, and the rest of it now hung in the balance. The ump yelled, "Play ball!"

and the press box echoed the sentiment. It was a common bitterness mixed with cheer.

He combed his hair. But still it was his mouth, and why did he do that? That little puckering motion out of nervous habit, constantly flexing his lips like he had been eating persimmons. It was a bona fide smirk, only he swore it wasn't. Who would he be smirking at, after all? What did he have to smirk about, with a measly dollar in his pocket? All the same, to everyone else it looked like a smirk and it affected them that way. A man walked over to him once and demanded belligerently, "Why are you looking at me that way? Wipe that stupid smile off your face."

"What stupid smile?" he replied.

"You know what smile, by God. You're still doing it."

And he wasn't even aware of it. It happened to him all the time, total strangers taking strong umbrage at something he was thinking. Imagine him trying to explain to them that it was just an innocent part of him, a little transmitter located in his lips that he wasn't even conscious of most of the time, sending out high frequency grief and tiny grin beams that got under people's skin and chafed their ass. To hear him tell it, it was totally hereditary and out of his hands, a hereditary smirk from a long line of thoroughbred smirkers, Irish thieves and storytellers, all no doubt smirking blissfully at this moment in the great beyond because he couldn't get back at them. But he could smirk, couldn't he? and that's who he was smirking at. No, not at this manjack or that one, not at some poor soul in this miserable fucked-up life, but at the whole setup. Johnny Boyle smirked at the universe. All great smirkers smirked at the universe, and going through World War II helped many a style. Whatever the reason, Johnny Boyle stood now at the pinnacle of his art, V-J Day, 1945.

A big band beat from the table radio in front of him prompted him to shift gears, as he rubbed Old Spice on his chin stubble and patted himself dry to 4/4 time. No doubt about it, it was great to be home, like he hadn't been gone a day. The Tommy Dorsey band was swinging like ever, Buddy De Franco on clarinet, Boomie Richman on tenor, Charlie Shavers, Buddy Rich from the U.S. Marines—these were the venerable elders of Johnny Boyle, the cats he grew up admiring like some kids followed the Yankees. He had known every band seating chart before the war, at least all the majors, the Dorseys, the Glenn Millers, the Benny Goodmans, the Count, Chick Webb, and so forth. Of course that wasn't so unusual. A whole generation grew up doing the same, following the big bands. But Boyle could tell you more. Not only could he tell you who played what for which outfit, he knew the arrangers, which tunes contained whose solos, the works. He read *Metronome* like it was manna from heaven, but he had his own opinions, too. He dumped all over the annual polls and used to lie awake nights thinking of ways to assassinate Sammy Kaye.

He picked up the radio and took a step before he remembered to unplug it, and even then the sound seemed to linger for a moment, the vibration still in the air as the song ended and Martin Block, originator of the "Make Believe Ballroom" over at WNEW, stepped up to a mike across town and got the real thing off on the right foot, putting it for everybody when he said, "The exaltation of it all! New York, V-J Day, the greatest party ever! What a night . . . the chaos and the confetti . . . the boys are coming home. In fact, a lot of them are here right now. This is yours truly Martin Block, coming to you live from the Moonlit Terrace at the beautiful Biltmore in downtown Manhattan. . . ."

The radio under his arm, he went out and cut the lights.

16

Peace at last! Johnny's brown-and-white Florsheims trampled the day's rubble underfoot and continued on their way up the littered sidewalk, stepping on broken glass and kicking liquor bottles aside. Among the delirious celebrants he attracted scant attention, though in other circumstances, in another place, he might have stopped traffic. Besides the bulky portable radio and the two-tone Florsheims, he sported a sport shirt that, like Boyle, was a true original, an aqua-blue configuration first spotted in a tourist trap on Forty-second Street next to Statue of Liberty ashtrays. He wore it in the style God intended, loose and outside the trousers, letting it billow in the breeze. On both front and back appeared an artist's rendering of the Empire State Building, surreal in its garish goldness, with darkened windows, in script beneath the legend *World's Tallest Building*. The two were a match, made for each other, and more than a few disoriented winos paused to observe him go past, following his progress with obvious envy.

They watched him pause as he went past a doorway on Eighth Avenue and came back for seconds, hearing some things he thought only *he* was hep to.

Already a crowd had gathered at the entrance, though at two steps below the sidewalk it wasn't much of a place, just a little jazz café like a spate of others soon to pop up in the neighborhood. But you couldn't miss the party inside. You had to come over and take a look, even if you didn't like the noise, because pretty soon they'd be calling the noise bebop, or bop for short.

This was 1945, you have to remember, and what Johnny heard there on the sidewalk sounded to most people like city traffic at rush hour if all the cars had different-pitched horns and weren't shy about using them. Something about nature and bebop both abhorred a vacuum, so you found notes in places you didn't know there were places. The drummer tried to squeeze as many beats into a bar as his motor nerves would permit, and the bass was always doing something you could never figure out, playing his own composition over in the corner, barely accommodating the others. But somehow there was something to it taken as a sum of its parts. Cymbals clashing, halftones and improvisation, a tenor sax probing the upper stratosphere—no wonder that most of the comments heard from Boyle's vantage point were derisive. It was still new, like the jet fighter.

He looked around at the people who were blocking the steps. Mostly they were vets, in and out of uniform, GI haircuts, too few dames to go around, intoxicated and laughing. Far worse, they didn't seem to be paying attention to the music, behavior which struck Boyle as nothing short of sacrilegious.

"Nice, huh?" he asked a vet in front of him. "Who's playing?"

The vet looked back at him in a hateful mood, surly beneath all the revelry.

"Bunch of baboons," he said. "Who knows?"

Johnny knew what the guy meant and had an impulse to slug him. The vet was obviously a smirker himself but without any class. The champ felt demeaned that they were even being seen together. The vet was drunk and with drunken friends. Otherwise Johnny was certain he would have straightened the jerk out, even to the point of starting something.

"You don't like the music?"

"What music? You call that music? I don't know why the hell they come down here. What's wrong with Harlem? Let 'em stay up there where they belong—"

It made sense to Boyle. After recognizing the vet's true nature, he didn't really expect much else. This wasn't the carefully orchestrated sweet sound of the big bands, with coordinated parts for sixteen guys. This

18

was syncopation, players playing to no rhythm but the ones they set for themselves, to each his own, free from polyrhythms, halving and doubling tempos as easily as you or I make change.

"Bunch of baboons."

So much for peacetime. America still had a thing or two on its mind, and Johnny had places to go, looking at his watch and turning to leave. As he did, he bumped into a slightly tipsy young blonde who for an instant appeared to be alone.

"Hey, watch where you're waltzing, you big galoot!" the blonde complained in the most strident way, squinting at him as though he were a street lamp. "Have you seen Herman?"

Obviously she had just been to the movies. "Watch where you're waltzing, you big galoot" was not ordinary speech even in 1945. It was of Hollywood origin, but he didn't mind. He wouldn't have minded being Herman either, for a night or two. The kid was cute, and sober she might have even been beautiful, although sober she never would have misplaced her glasses and be squinting so, the size of a pixie with a little upturned nose. Johnny thought there were plenty of guys who would be willing to help her home, and presently several appeared in the form of one. He was Herman, the world's fattest Marine, and he too had a little upturned nose. It seemed they were a brother-sister act, and she and Johnny weren't meant to be, this night or any other.

Fortune wasn't with them, and it was to be a similarly cruel night for millions, although to save face Johnny did manage to get in a word or two before they drifted on their separate ways forever.

"Good evening, my name is Johnny Boyle," he said, sincere, polite. "I find you a very charming young lady and am desirous of the pleasure of your conversation. I'm staying at present—"

19

She wasn't impressed, and neither was Herman. Little else mattered. The crowd pressed her and Johnny together for a second, but she wasn't interested. He watched her walk away unsteadily with Herman, her ankles collapsing in her high heels.

Losing her made life bitter, a fact he announced to those around him, to anyone who would bother to listen. Hardly anyone did.

"How d'ya like that? Stuck-up broad," he said. "Did you see that? What're ya, stuck-up?"

He called after her, and in Pittsburgh he might have gotten an audience. But here in New York he was just another waltzing galoot, another sidewalk character. He shrugged it off and moved on. There wasn't time to dwell on the failures. After all, this was V-J Day, and all over Gotham a thousand similar vignettes were taking place, each without any awareness of the others, under the fireworks, spotlights, and the neon sky. *Coca-Cola, Wrigley's Spearmint, Admiral,* and all the other arsenals of democracy—a million signs, a million stories. The world was safe again. The blonde had even looked Jewish.

The night was young, and five minutes later Johnny struck again, this time in a hock shop just up the street. The middle-aged proprietor tending a regular customer looked up at the sound of a radio blaring and excused himself. Across the room Johnny had plugged in and was tapping his Florsheims on tile in time with a few choice words, exhorting the vacuum tubes to perform better in the same way he might talk to live musicians. All of this had its effect on the proprietor, who had lost an honor student on Guam.

"You wanted something?" the man asked him with a frown.

"Yeah, how're you doing?" Johnny said with his most inoffensive smile. "I wanna show you this radio. I think you'll get a kick out of it. By far the finest I ever

20

heard, built by the same people who built the bomb-sight."

"Bombsights I can move," the proprietor said, a sense of humor grown weary. "Four bucks, take it or leave it."

The radio itself was no great shakes, but Johnny thought he could beat four dollars. He polished the varnish with his shirt, concentrating on the scratches and the carved names of previous owners, preferring to ignore the first and final offer. Instead, he got hysteri-cal, waving his arms, manipulating the volume and turning knobs like a Toscanini, catching smatterings of a dozen different broadcasts in the radio capital of the world, using each to strengthen his pitch.

"Listen to that. You hear that?" he said. "It gets Benny Goodman. And it gets the Andrews Sisters un-believably well. Tommy Dorsey. Hear that? Great breath control. He's over at the Biltmore this very minute—I'm going over there to see him myself in a few minutes—and all through the magic of the Mar-coni. Edward R. Murrow. The Duke. Cab Calloway. This here radio even gets the President of the United States, Harry S. Truman—"

The proprietor stood his ground. "Four bucks. My tops," he said, starting to move away before Johnny gently drew him back.

"And speaking of Sinatra," he went on, "the shrimp don't sound this good even in the shower. Frankie boy ain't even skinny on this radio."

He made his point, but there was no point. None of it was going to get him anywhere, and the proprietor had heard enough. He yanked the cord out of the elec-trical socket and handed the whole apparatus back to Johnny, leading him routinely by the elbow toward the front door, Johnny's protests no more effective than his sales delivery had been.

"Lookit, Pops, you heard of V-J Day, right?" he

21

said, intended to appeal for sympathy, that old standby when all else failed, for God and country. "You got a subscription, you go outta the shop from time to time. Outside this hock shop, the world's safe for democracy again. The war's over, Audie Murphy's coming home. So have a heart, Pops. Be a citizen, help a vet usher in the peace."

But to the pawnbroker who had lost a son, it all sounded too too familiar. He'd heard it all before, all day long, and his grip was firm. "The peace comes in, you go out. Go. Go on. I've seen one too many GI's today. Soldiers, sailor boys, you're all the same. You come to the city for a wild time, you got no money."

"I noticed that already."

"Keep your radio and stay out of New York. Take my advice, war hero—go home to Kansas, wherever it is you come from."

"I'm from Pitt," Boyle said, the proprietor pushing him the few final inches out the door and closing it behind him.

"Pittsburgh, then," the proprietor said through the glass as he turned the keys in the several locks. "Go home to Pittsburgh, that's my advice. Get a job before the others come home." He said this as he pulled the shade down and hung a simple sign toward the street, *Closed for the holiday.* Johnny of course rejected the voice of experience out of hand, heading instead for the next pawnshop.

There followed immediately an explosion of big band music that seemed to come from the mysterious dark mouth of a gold trombone, the instrument in familiar hands, the ring on the pinkie, the slide extended. CLOSE ON TROMBONE, PULL BACK TO REVEAL the late, great Tommy Dorsey. But he wasn't late in those days, this leader for a decade of the greatest dance band ever. You could argue the point—there were a lot of great outfits around over the years when big bands held sway, but none of the others could do as many things as well as Tommy Dorsey's crew. (Big bands were always called crews or aggregations.) These cats could swing with style and hold a mood all night, and nobody played a better ballad. Remember "For Sentimental Reasons"? That was Tommy Dorsey. Or "Little White Lies"? "You Taught Me How to Love Again"? No? There were dozens of others, all with that sentimental horn of his and the work of great sidemen and vocalists such as Jo Stafford and the greatest of them all, a fellow named Sinatra. "My Prayer"? "Embraceable You"? "Everything Happens to Me"? "There Are Such Things"?

Still don't remember? Then you missed it, that's all, and worse, you don't know what you missed. But now's as good a time to start as any. If you've never seen or heard a big band except at a football game, you're in trouble. You have to use your imagination because big bands, as they used to exist, don't exist any more. To young people they're prehistoric, and to the old crowd they're nostalgic, which must mean they don't exist any more. Not three or four middle-aged teen-agers yelling their brains out to be heard over their own feedback, but upward of sixteen grown men in three rows all dressed alike in any color you might name, as long as it was red, white or blue, sometimes sitting, sometimes springing to their feet in a moment of frenzy, shouting unintelligibles in unison and swinging their instruments like cavemen, this way and that, up at the ceiling, all in time to the music and without losing a beat. In Tommy Dorsey's band, the guys in the front row even had their own glee club. When they got tired of playing, they could always sing, turning in choruses on such Dorsey standards as "Marie."

It looked like half of New York had managed to shoehorn its way into the Biltmore that evening, into a

23

great old room called the Moonlit Terrace, a fairyland
sort of place under a canopy of stars. White linen and
candlelight, khaki uniforms and tuxedos, it reminded
Boyle of London, Pfc's rubbing noses and private parts
with the aristocracy. While the envious watched on the
sidelines, the lucky ones danced. This was the USA of
legend, not record, and for one night it all made sense.
It all hung together. That was war, this was peace.
You're you, and I'm me. Now is now and then is then.
Like that. There were simple answers to everything.
Spotlights scanned the floor, and those caught in the
glow had strangely frozen expressions, a catalogue of
the times. Where are they today? I wonder.

But Boyle wasn't thinking any of this. As the
Tommy Dorsey number came to its rousing conclusion
amid the merrymaking, the crowd shouted its pleasure,
and Johnny Boyle took a bow as the spotlight finally
found him. When the light moved on, he resumed his
trek through flesh, looking for a face he knew.

On the bandstand, Tommy Dorsey stepped over to
join Martin Block at the WNEW microphone. Block's
voice was a little hoarse tonight, but it wasn't because
his bow tie was on too tight. Things were loud and getting no better.

"Well, Tommy," Block said for the thousands of lis-
teners at home, "this is the first Lucky Strike peacetime
broadcast in almost four years, and I must say the
Tommy Dorsey musical aggregation has never sounded
better."

"Thanks, Marty," Dorsey said, "but it'd be awfully
hard not to be at our best on a night like tonight. It's a
great feeling, believe me."

You couldn't argue with success, and after a few
more words at the mike, which hardly anyone heard,
Dorsey relented and the band swung into "Marie," the
song they were all calling for. You could tell from
the cheer it got. Boyle couldn't hear anything, but the

24

whole madhouse started to sing. When he finally could hear, it was a familiar voice shouting his name.

"Hey, Johnny! Maestro! Over here!"

He turned on a dime to see a quartet of soldiers just a few feet away, all uniformly dressed and uniformly inebriated. They were the Musketeers, what was left of them, the four of them tottering like the sea of people around them, soldiers, sailors, everyone singing the lyrics to "Marie" as boisterously as possible, welcoming Johnny into the fold with handshakes and laughter, the most vocal among them being a red-haired kid from the South named Alabama.

"Johnny, sonofabitch, where you been? Where's your uniform?"

They called him Alabama, as it was more polite than calling him Loony, which was his real name in more ways than one. He was one of the original Musketeers (384th Bomb Group, "We bombed Big B and lived," March of '44), a guy in every outfit, like Kowalski in the war movies. When the moon was full, he told stories stretched out on the ground, he had spent much of the war lying under tables. He had a tattoo to show for it and seemed never to protest. He just did his job, a lumbering good ole boy from Dixie. Most of the war was all right with him.

Next to him was Jackpot, who for some reason thought he was Johnny's best friend, a misinterpretation that over the years encroached on everything. Tonight he was feeling especially sentimental and he pulled Johnny's head to his breast, stroking his hair like a pussycat.

"Johnny, where's your uniform?"

To a man, they seemed hurt he hadn't worn it.

"I hocked it," he said, looking around, taking the joint in. "Jackpot, where's our table? Where're the broads?"

It would have been a farcical question for anyone

25

except Boyle to ask. It was perfectly apparent that there were at least ten anxious individuals for every seat in the house, but these were mere technicalities that never registered with Boyle. There was such a thing as native birthright, and he didn't consider himself human anyway. Still, Jackpot's words had their sobering effect.

"What broads? You guys seen any broads? We ain't got nothing, as in zero. DiMuzio couldn't come through—they can't make it."

"*Can't fucking make it?*" Johnny couldn't believe it, that it was happening to him. "For chrissake, not on V-J Day! You're shitting me—we ain't striking out on V-J Day! Where is the bastard? I'll kill him. I ain't getting stiffed like this—this is garbage."

"So tell him," Jackpot said. "He's here."

"Where?"

Jackpot said something, but Johnny didn't hear. The decibel count rose at the same time he felt something cold and liquid pour over his head. Whirling around, he saw a smiling stranger with an empty glass of champagne in one hand. It was a simple mistake anyone could have made. He had doused Johnny, thinking him someone else.

"Sorry, you're not Herman," he said and walked off, as Johnny's jaw dropped.

"Herman? Who the fuck's Herman?" he mumbled.

"How's the music business?" Alabama yelled in his ear. "Making any encores? Did you hear I'm pulling out tonight?"

Johnny hadn't heard and didn't care to hear, getting hotter by the minute—first the personal affront by the dames from Jersey who weren't showing up, and now the champagne slowly trickling down his collar. "Where's DiMuzio? Where is he?"

Alabama pointed. "You see that tall blonde down front?"

26

Barely, but he saw her, a tall blonde in a WAC cap bobbing head and shoulders above the others near the bandstand.

"The Viking?"

"Right. Locate her tits, and you've found DiMuzio." It was a straightforward way of putting it, and DiMuzio was a straightforward guy. Tall tits seemed the perfect hiding place, and Johnny nodded, shoving off at once, though much too soon to suit Alabama, who still didn't think he fully understood. "Johnny, I'm leaving tonight!" he said.

Boyle had already vanished in the crush of people, and Alabama felt sure they would one day see each other again, but he was wrong. Those were the last words they would ever say to one another. Alabama went home and was soon killed in an argument over an automobile.

Back on the bandstand, the musicians were standing idly by, watching the phenomenal young drummer Buddy Rich. And some work the kid from Brooklyn was doing, hands moving like pile drivers to the naked eye, hail and thunder in a scrawny package. For some reason people always want to cheer drum solos before they're finished. Maybe it's a leftover from passion rites, but that night was no exception. Rich had barely gotten underway and the applause was already building, as he twirled his sticks between his fingers.

One of those in the audience who didn't clap at once was a young woman sitting at ringside at one of the choicer tables. She was alone, or at least gave the impression. To dispense with the formalities, because that's the way she was, her name was Francine Evans. Maybe it rings a bell. If it doesn't, you've been away a long time, like institutionalized the past twenty-five years or so. You'd have had to be to miss her. Meaning, nowadays you can't just pick up the phone and dial her direct. You have to go through MCA, and they put you in touch with CMI or IFA, or is it ICM now? In other words, it's not easy. But in those days, anybody could walk up to her and put in his two cents' worth, and "anybody" went for even Johnny Boyle.

The reason she wasn't clapping was because she was listening. She was a helluva listener, a talent that would later come in handy with Boyle, who could always give you an earful. Beyond that, she listened to a lot of music and knew what to listen for. She could even play pretty fair drums herself, so Buddy Rich's solo held more than her mild attention. She was tapping a pair of swizzle sticks on a cocktail glass when Boyle approached from the rear.

He didn't say anything to her at first, and she didn't see him. He looked at her twice and almost had second thoughts about the whole thing, about even opening his mouth—it had been that kind of day, and the fact was, she didn't look his type. He preferred blondes, and she was brunette. At least the part of her hair he could see looked brunette. The rest of it was stuffed under a brown WAC cap and her figure didn't come off much better, her more prominent points camouflaged by the lumpy uniform she wore. Besides her own drink there was a cocktail glass on the table that looked as if it had been sitting there unattended for some time. The ice in it was melting, and maybe Boyle was thirsty. Maybe that's what went through his cryptic mind, who knows? At any rate, when the drum solo ended, he made his move.

"Don't I know you from someplace?"

She didn't even hear him. The whole brass section had all at once jumped in at the end of the drums and was playing terrific, Boyle himself looking to the bandstand, as she turned to see him kneeling beside her chair. It was a momentous occasion, a formidable encounter. There he was, sticking a fresh stick of gum in his mouth, his hair champagne-plastered over his forehead, their eyes meeting for the first time in their lives. He decided to repeat the question until he got a reaction, one way or another.

"Don't I know you from someplace?"

"No," she said, and it was the first time he realized that when she looked at you, she was prettier than when you looked at her. There was just something special on the inside, and we've all met the type. The icing on the plain cookie. She just looked different when she turned those brown eyes on you. You didn't forget her, and in the retelling afterward, you'd swear she had been gorgeous. It was such a pleasant surprise, and he had walked over expecting so little, that he was temporarily at a loss.

"I know you from someplace." It was all he could think of.

"No."

"I do know you from someplace. Listen—excuse me, can you look at me for a minute? I'm not putting you on. My parents—my mother and father, my brother and sister are over there on the other side. I just got out of the service."

"Where are they?"

"They're on the other side over there. I got to spend time with them. But I know you from someplace—I'm not kidding, we met somewhere."

"No."

"No, we did meet somewhere. I'm not putting you on. I'm serious. I got no time to put you on, I'm not putting you on. I'm serious. Can I get your phone number and I'll call you tomorrow morning and I'll explain what it is. I know you and I got something I want to tell you . . . I know what it is. Okay?"

"No."

"What is it? Can I get your phone number?"

"No."

"Can I call you? Can I meet you someplace?"

"No. No."

"Can I call you at work?"

"No."

"There's no way at all?"

"No."

"There's no way at all?"

"No. This seat is taken."

"Yeah, I know. I'm just trying to sit here and think of another angle."

"Skip it. I've heard every angle I'll ever hear tonight."

"How about this one—swinging band, huh?"

She groaned, picked up his line and finished it for him. "Really swings," she said.

"Really swings." He nodded.

"No, really," she said. "I don't mean to be rude, but the seat is taken. I'm here with some friends."

"I'll leave as soon as they come back."

"Why don't you leave right now?"

"Because I don't wanna leave right now. I wanna talk to you. If I leave right now, I'll never get to meet you. I'll never get to know what a wonderful, beautiful girl you are. You and I could reach new heights and planes . . . I'm not putting you on. Do you know what I'm saying? We can relate on a higher level."

"Shows what you know," she mumbled.

"USO?"

"No, I said, 'Shows what you know.' "

"What shows do I know?"

"I don't know," she said.

He continued in the same vein, speaking very peculiarly, champagne dripping down to the corner of his mouth where he caught it with a flick of his tongue.

"Anyway, I thought you might wanna dance—be desirous, so to speak, if I'm not being intrusive—you know what I mean."

"Oh, but you are being intrusive. I turned around

and you were in my face. The minute I laid eyes on you, I looked at you and thought, 'intrusive.' "

"Oh, I see, I am being 'intrusive.' "

"Yes. Why don't you just go someplace else and try it again?"

No problem. He got up and walked away, only to return immediately. He sat down again.

"Who was that guy in the Hawaiian shirt and white pants?" he said with a perfectly straight face. "Was he bothering you? Looked like a crazy person to me."

"Not crazy, just pushy."

A pause.

"You know what he said about you over there?" he asked.

"What?"

"Nothing."

She laughed. "That's what I thought."

"How about giving me a big whopping kiss," he said, "for V-J Day."

"Well, no. Would you settle for a split lip?"

They both gave phony laughs, like it had been a phony conversation from beginning to end, and it had. But still they went on. Boyle kept at it, and she checked her watch.

"You know, when I was over there, walking toward you," he began, "I realized I fought the war for a reason. Yes, when I was in my foxhole, sweating and fighting, thinking any minute might be my last, not knowing when I'd see this country again, I kept wondering if I was just a part of something grander, bigger, and I didn't know. But back there, the first time I saw you, I knew."

"Knew what?"

"Knew that I wasn't going to get anywhere at this table."

"Now I'm impressed," she said.

To an extent she meant it. If it hadn't been for that

31

smirk of his, she might have asked him to pull up a chair. But that look ... it gave her the willies, that look emanating not from his eyes but from his mouth. A woman would have to be crazy to get involved with a man like that. He looked positively carnivorous.

"Well, I guess a little small talk is in order here," he said.

"Can it get any smaller? Can you also take a walk?"

"Hey, I can take a hint. Is that it? Very funny, very funny. You want me to leave, right?"

Silence.

"You're right," he said, his eyes darting about as if he were claustrophobic. "How about this place? I feel like a bay leaf in a windstorm. I'm looking for a friend of mine, sort of short paesano, stocky, armed and dangerous, last seen dancing with a seven-foot Amazon."

"Would that be him over there? The one with the eyebrows?"

He looked where she pointed and saw once again the tall blonde WAC and the not-so-visible corporal she was dancing with, the two of them in an intense bear hug, oblivious to the rest of the world. She was Ellen Flanery, and he of wavy hair and dimpled chin stuck deep in her cleavage was Eddie DiMuzio, Johnny Boyle's favorite Musketeer until tonight. Now he wasn't so sure, depending on how his luck held the rest of the evening. Eddie was looking over and waving, calling on Johnny and Francine to join them.

"Looks like you've found him," Francine said.

"Yeah, that's him." It had become rather obvious he wasn't actually looking for anyone at all, and he shifted his weight back uncomfortably.

"That's your first little lie," she said, disillusioned with him suddenly, with the world in general. "I was really starting to like you, and then you say something like that. You might have had your way if you'd just told the truth. Why do people always feel compelled to do that?"

"Do what?" he said, quickly on the defensive.

"You know what," she said. "Give alibis. Why do people always have to hide behind alibis? If you wanted to dance, why didn't you just come over here and say so? Just say, 'Do you wanna dance?' "

He looked at her, racking his brain. Out of habit he pointed back at Eddie. "They said—that girl with my friend over there—that you might wanna shake out the soot—"

"Don't bring Ellen into it. I know her too well, and she wouldn't interfere with what I wanted to do. Anyway, you just did it again! Another alibi. Do you wanna dance or don't you?"

He was more confounded than ever, still unwilling to drop his guard. "They said you might be—"

"Desirous of dancing?" she said, finishing the sentence for him. "Leave them out of it. Are you gonna ask me to dance or not?"

Finally he said, "Do you wanna dance?"

"No," she said.

Just like that. No. What a sense of humor. He looked like he'd been shot. This couldn't be happening. He licked his lips and began all over again.

"They thought you might wanna shake out the soot, that's all," he said. "You've been sitting over here by yourself all night."

"Oh. Feeling sorry for me?"

"Sort of, yeah."

That was it, as far as she was concerned. She felt let down and yet in a way relieved. For a minute there she had been on the verge of actually dancing with this guy, a guy she might have gotten to know and like, and that made no sense for someone in her position who didn't even know how long she would be in town or

33

any of the rest of it. So, yeah, she felt relieved to find him petty and irritable and not at all her type.

"I'm sorry, I'm more desirous of sitting here right now," she said. "I'm not much for shaking out the soot. I just spent a couple of nights on a lumpy mattress, and I'm really very tired."

"You oughtta try my place," he said, extending a stick of Juicy Fruit.

"And I'm getting even tireder of you."

He was undeterred. Having nothing to lose, he grew bolder, for some reason still wagging the protruding stick of chewing gum in an empty package, until it dawned on her he was making an obscene gesture. He was still offering her gum, wiggling it, despite the fact that she continued to glare at him.

"I mean, what's the point of winning the goddamn war if you can't carouse a little on V-J Day?" he said. "You know what I mean?"

It wasn't hard to guess. "Try a Hershey bar," she said. "Isn't that what you mean?"

He stood there, trying to think of a topper, wishing he could reach in his pocket and pull out a Hershey bar that very moment. He'd like to see the look on her face then, then realized how silly it was. They were glowering at each other, and someone had to say something. Someone had to accept responsibility for turning a casual proposition into a contest of wills. He didn't, but thought it might be a nice gesture if he apologized first, before she had the chance.

"Lookit, nothing personal—" he started to say.

"Nothing personal, that's just your problem. We're all the same to you. Better luck next time. Goodbye."

She hadn't minced words. Boyle wasn't one to walk away, however, without having the last say. It would be tantamount to admitting defeat, and to stave that off, at least, he said cockily, "Well, I'll take a rain check then. Maybe the next war?"

"What makes you think you'll win the next one?" she said, the last say hers, without even looking at him. She looked instead toward the bandstand, where the band was breaking for intermission. Several of the musicians were already headed her way, one of them waving in a jovial mood.

"Evans! Hey, Evans!"

Johnny fumed at her, fumed at the musicians, and astonished himself by feeling a twinge of jealousy, his smirk tightening. He could think of absolutely nothing to say as the red jackets closed in and shut him out.

"Evans!" several of them shouted, arriving and pumping her hand. "Evans, long time no see, for crying out loud! Remember me? Ernie!"

She accepted their handshakes, trying to put names with faces. It hadn't been that long ago, but it seemed ages, another part of her left back there somewhere on the winding road.

"Ernie! And—?"

"Remember me?"

"Troy."

"Arnold!" Arnold corrected. "Paul's friend from Fort Devon."

Chapter 3

PAUL. SHE HADN'T SEEN PAUL SINCE . . . THEIR SPLIT. She wondered how he was, practically her favorite steady companion on the three-year tour, and now she hadn't thought of him in months. She'd gotten a card from him at Christmas.

Looking over Arnold's shoulder, she saw the Juicy Fruit Kid trying desperately to get her attention. If nothing else, he was persistent. She could say that much for him, watching him as he sarcastically panned all the names mentioned, moving his lips—"Ernie, Troy, Arnold, Paul," going through a whole rigmarole. He looked like a four-year-old, and she did her best to ignore him, though occasionally keeping tabs on him out of the corner of her eye as he decided finally to withdraw, causing her to smile in spite of herself as the *World's Tallest Building* faded into the sunset. To herself, she wondered where a guy like that got off, much less ended up.

"Ray Bolger Show, Christmas last! Where were you, Evans?" someone asked, swallowing her cocktail olive without waiting to be asked.

"My mother died," she said.

"I'm sorry."

"Not as sorry as she was." No point in being morbid.

And they broke out laughing, another hand reaching for the unattended drink.

"Was she old?"

"Not as old as she wanted to be."

"Hey, Evans! You're still terrific! Don't ever change! You hear me, Evans? Don't ever change—" Some of them left the table now, parched throats in search of greener pastures, leaving just her and Paul's friend Arnold, the latter a compulsive grabber and manic depressive. He was clutching her hand.

"T.D. just asked me back aboard last week. I just got out. No kidding, Evans, you should have come with us to London. Some great high jinks if you'd been there—"

"I was afraid that old bus wouldn't make it."

"You mean across the Atlantic?"

That's what she meant, and he went limp as jelly, laughing his head off and grabbing her. "Hey, that's funny! Hey, no kidding, Evans—don't ever lose your sense of humor! See you later."

She called after him, "How's Paul, anyway?"

Arnold turned, had a perfect blank expression. "Paul?"

"Your friend Paul from Fort Devon, my friend and yours—"

"Oh, Paul—he's here! Yeah, in New York. I saw him yesterday. He's got something lined up. How about you?"

"Well, I don't know. I'm not really sure."

"Hey, don't ever change, Evans—always modest. I love it."

And with that he turned, bumping into several tables on his way up the aisle. She surmised he'd had his fingers in the medicine cabinet, if he was the same one she remembered. He was shaking more hands as he made his way, and she wished him the best. As for herself, she was feeling more or less depressed, sleepier and lonesome suddenly.

Then, as she was slipping her purse over her shoulder and preparing to leave, she saw *him* again. Just what he was up to over there on the other side of the dance floor was unclear. Standing by a table and watching a smartly dressed woman walk away from him in the company of her high society escort, Mr. Juicy Fruit appeared to have been stiff-armed a second time in as many tries, again left in the lurch.

The woman did find him amusing, however, and left him with this farewell piece of advice. "Never say die." She smiled. "Stay off the junk and you'll go far."

On that note she retreated, and Johnny now turned his gaze on Francine across the floor. Both still alone, they regarded each other for a few seconds, and Martin Block's voice came over the microphone.

"More of the band at ten, ladies and gentlemen. A short pause—" When Johnny looked at the popular

37

MC and then looked back to where she had been, she was gone. He spotted only a glimpse of her later and thought of following her home like a figure in the shadows, but Eddie DiMuzio arrived first, pulling him over for a heart-to-heart, DiMuzio as bubbly as the champagne his head was swimming in, coming up gasping for air.

"Johnny, sweetheart, a small favor to ask—" That was the way DiMuzio always talked: "Sweetheart," "Sugar," "Darling," very smooth even when he was desperate, and tonight he was desperate. "I'm in love since half an hour. I got a feeling this girl's a Broadway dancer, Johnny—chorus-line type, extremely leggy—you know what that means. You using your room key tonight? I wouldn't ask except I gotta go somewhere to control my urges. She's more anxious than I am, and it's making me nervous."

Something was making him nervous. It had to be the real thing. It couldn't be all sheer hallucination, the way his heart was pounding, his eyes looking at Johnny as a last hope, and under the circumstances, what could Johnny do but help a pal? He dug deep.

"I need a phone number," he said, and maybe he should have left well enough alone. It was embarrassing how eager DiMuzio would have complied with any request, how he fished his most precious possession out of his pocket and presented it to Johnny without a moment's hesitation, pausing only long enough to flip the pages so he could hear the breeze rustle through them a final time. It was his little black book, a World War Two classic, carefully compiled and kept up-to-date over the years, carried next to his heart in battle and treasured above all. Yet he handed it over gladly.

"You kidding me?" he said. "For you, anything. Sky's the limit, babe. I'll give you my whole little black book, names, info—and it's all for you. I don't need it 'cause I just met the woman of my dreams. This baby's got the hottest numbers in New York with an appendix for Jersey."

"Yeah, but it ain't got the one I want."

"Yeah, who's that?" DiMuzio couldn't believe there was one he'd overlooked, but he had. Francine wasn't in the book.

A couple of hours later, a sleepy hand reached for an ivory-colored telephone ringing in the dark. The bare arm belonged to Francine, who rolled over in bed and sat up, surprised, and yet not really, to find herself looking at four strange walls. After all, it happened daily. For a minute she couldn't place herself for the life of her, and then she remembered. "Hotel room. New York. And that's my phone ringing."

Her hand picked it up without further instructions from the brain, and the ringing stopped. She raised the receiver to her ear and got something of a shock, like someone had placed a mad buzzer in her palm on the pretense of a handshake. "Whazzit—Hershey bar?" the voice at the other end said as she hung up in a hurry, dumping the phone in its cradle, then thinking about it afterward. A minute later it rang again, and when it stopped this time, she called the desk and asked them to hold all calls. The odd character she had met at the Biltmore, she thought. Who else but him? Odd but handsome around the mouth in a disconcerting way, and by now she was awake and could think of nothing else.

The hotel bed was suddenly too soft, and she turned restlessly, thinking she would be lucky if she could get back to sleep at all tonight, and yet she couldn't really be angry. You couldn't be angry at a crazy person, and that's what he obviously was, obviously needing help and understanding. She tried to get him out of her mind, that insipid smile of his.

She had meant to call Tony, her agent, today, and

hadn't. There hadn't been time, but that was a lie, she told herself. There was always time for a phone call. Anyway, why the fuss? He knew she was arriving today, didn't he? She was certain she had mentioned the date, and even if she hadn't he would know where she was staying; he could always call and check to see if she had come into town yet. Why did she always have to be the one to do everything? She knew she was rationalizing, and yet that's how she felt half the time, and now she had to go to sleep. Why did she always have to be the one to go to sleep? She was tired of being so responsible. Maybe it was time she did something irresponsible for once.

She shut her eyes, counting iambic pentameter instead of sheep. What had that guy said his name was, the crazy guy at the Moonlit Terrace?

Chapter 4

ACROSS TOWN JIMMY STEWART WAS STEPPING OUT OF a phone booth. He had just called June Allyson back in Colorado and asked her to come to New York to marry him. It was a big decision on their part, and their connection unfortunately wasn't the best. But it worked out fine in the long run. He had to repeat the number he was calling from and inadvertently discovered the title for a song he was going to write in her honor a few minutes later in *The Glenn Miller Story*. It was "Pennsylvania 6–5000," one of the all-time great big band numbers. If you want to know where all the old songs went, there's your answer. Ask your phone company if they've heard of "736–5000" lately. That's where the songs went. That's where we are today.

Meanwhile, it's a wonder Boyle's path and Jimmy

Stewart's didn't cross at least once that night, because Boyle, too, stepped out of a phone booth, and he looked twice the musician Jimmy Stewart was. He carried a copy of *Variety* under one arm, and in his torrid sport shirt stood in contrast to the drab backdrop of elevated trains rumbling through the night, past the old tenements. He had no particular plan of attack, but had already lost five nickels in the transaction, trying to phone Francine but not getting through, owing to some sort of mix-up. He was convinced the failure was mechanical, and he'd try again tomorrow. He might even go over, drop in unannounced, though he had to guard against appearing too anxious, or in a hurry to apologize. Probably it would be better if he called, using some casual excuse. He had an unabridged personality, and the smirk had cost him dearly tonight. The minute he had smirked, she had noticed it. He had been doing fine until then. Besides, people told him he was downright personable over the phone.

He switched his *Variety* to the other hand, and as he turned to walk, an odd sight across the street caught his eye, a haunting image that would remain with him for some time. A sailor and a young woman were dancing below the tracks of the El, performing a Ginger Rogers–Fred Astaire routine with a quick flourish of moves for no one but themselves, the sailor lifting the woman off the ground and spinning her once in the air before he caught her, their shoes echoing on the concrete.

They were magnificent, and the longer he watched them, the more persistently a musical composition began to steal its way into his thoughts and the more he walked erratically. He was hearing the first bars of a song that would one day be called "New York, New York." That's the main reason he didn't run into Jimmy Stewart that night, because unlike the latter,

41

Johnny wasn't Glenn Miller and didn't know where he was going.

Boyle was convinced that music was out to kill him. Perhaps that's why he chose to zigzag from curb to curb that night through the streets of Manhattan and through most of his life, rambling like a lost soul trying to shake off a demon. Only it never worked. He would discover himself playing a tune on his fingers without even being aware of it, bringing all his New Year's resolutions to ruin. Music had his number, and dodging the question wouldn't cure the impulse. It had to be resolved one way or another, and in the meantime the monkey on his back waylaid him at every opportunity, put odd noises in his head in place of the cup of human kindness, and in general didn't make life any easier, including where to sleep in New York on V-J Day at three in the morning.

The next anyone saw of him, he was walking down Lexington in broad daylight, blinking and with bags under his eyes. If he had slept at all, his face gave no sign of it, a shadow of beard obscuring whatever else was there. He didn't look either way, just kept walking, through the revolving door of the Waldorf-Astoria, watching his Florsheims eat up the carpet, left-right, left-right, into the lobby like a zombie.

If he had slept, he might have dreamed it, but he never would have guessed it. One of life's smug coincidences played out for his benefit, and even so, he didn't see her at first. He was too busy padding his steps. His hands were thrust into his pockets in search of a casual stride, and the copy of *Variety* was gripped snugly between ribs and elbow. He was moving across the lobby, down on his luck from the night before, but his smirk hadn't diminished. On the contrary, in inverse proportion to his success, it often grew.

Across the way, standing at the main desk and talking in spirited tones with the desk clerk, was Francine Evans. "New and improved," as Madison Avenue would say. In marked contrast to him, she looked as though a night's sleep had done her a world of good. She was freshly scrubbed and groomed, civilian style, wearing something in polka dots.

She was saying, "She *isn't* registered. That's what I'm telling you. She's with a friend, a close friend. Do you understand?"

Desk clerks never understand such things, not even the morning after V-J Day. They always sleep at home alone.

"She called me, asked me to meet her here, but she wasn't feeling well and couldn't remember the room number. But the name is Johnny something-or-other—she's in Johnny's room."

"Johnny's room?"

"I'm worried, see. I'm afraid it might be her malaria. It clobbers her when she drinks too much—"

At the mention of the dreaded malaria, the clerk's interest quickened for the first time.

"Malaria? If you'll pardon me—" he said.

He started to take a step and she said, "Never mind. I see him now. That's him."

She referred to Johnny Boyle, the fellow in the shirt, who, even now as they observed him, ambled over to the bank of elevators, unaware of the fate about to befall him. Since he hadn't been looking, he had seen no trouble afoot, but it was there nonetheless in the squinted eyes of the desk clerk, who had had special instructions regarding Mr. Boyle in 1106. He had been meaning to have a little talk with Boyle, and after he had cast an especially sour look in that direction, he thought it prudent to call his immediate superior, Mr. Parkins, without delay.

"Oh, Mr. Parkins—"

Mr. Parkins came over and the two of them huddled

behind the counter. Francine's curiosity was aroused. With all due urgency, Parkins picked up the house microphone and held it poised, watching his quarry. In fact, the three of them watched, studying closely Boyle's reaction for a sign of guilt when he heard his name come over the public-address system.

"Paging Mr. Boyle," Parkins said with relish. He liked to make them squirm, his lips touching the cold steel. "Will you please step to the main desk, Mr. Boyle?"

But Boyle's face indicated nothing, like he hadn't heard. He didn't turn around, didn't move his head. What he did do was press the elevator button in somewhat of a hurry. Parkins in turn reacted like he had a fish flopping on the hook, excited by the scent of blood. He repeated, "Over here, Mr. Boyle. Please turn to your left. We're to the left of the elevators."

Faced with no alternative, Boyle turned and executed well. He looked quizzical as he pointed to himself, wondering if they could possibly mean him.

"Yes, you, Mr. Boyle," said Parkins and hung up the mike, but not before he had already generated a good deal of interest among the spectators in the lobby. By now, practically all the lounge-chair readers had lowered their papers and were looking at Boyle, amused that such heavy artillery as the P.A. system had been used at such close range on one so seemingly undistinguished, guilty only of banality. At least that was the look Boyle had as the elevator landed and the doors opened. He hesitated for a moment, considering whether to make a run for it or face the music. It might be something else entirely, for all he knew. He knew better, but it was just possible. Anyway, the elevator doors now closed without him, and that was that. He ambled over.

"Could I speak with you a moment, Mr. Boyle?" Parkins said, as the clerk slipped him a folder containing the pertinent information. "There appears to have been some misunderstanding, but it shouldn't take long to get cleared away."

Boyle mustered his most indignant voice. "I hope not," he said. "I'm a busy man."

"Yes, I can see that."

Parkins was looking inside the folder, and Boyle was looking at Francine suddenly, as though just now connecting her to last night. He was talking to Parkins, but his eyes were on her. "What's the big stink anyhow? I ain't even turned in. I been out all night watching the Three Stooges."

"Hello, Juicy Fruit," she said. No one asked her, but she jumped in anyway, making a gratuitous comment with a smile, thinking the whole thing highly entertaining. "A likely story, Inspector," she said to Parkins. "Is it OK if I go up now?"

"Just a moment, please," Parkins said, examining a matter of record in the folder. She wasn't going anywhere anyway, at least not for the time being. Boyle had his foot over hers, and she was working to free herself, though doing her best not to draw attention. Nevertheless, several in the armchair gallery continued to watch the proceedings with care. They would turn a page and look back, maybe reading an editorial, then check the latest in Johnny and Francine's jockeying for position out of Parkins' view.

Boyle was watching Parkins sift through the papers and detected no inclination on the latter's part to listen to a word he might say. If he had to mumble to someone, it might as well be her, and she looked extraordinary this morning, her hair worn loose. He said under his breath, and it was true, "I didn't recognize you out of your khakis. What's the matter, your battle ribbons get too heavy for you? Weighing you down a little bit? You gotta come over here and mess me up—"

"Where's Ellen?" she said.

He didn't answer that one, looking on as the situation behind the desk swiftly deteriorated. Beside Parkins, the desk clerk had now picked up the telephone and was speaking into it in a low voice, not taking his eyes off Johnny. Johnny remained cool, his nonetheless clammy hand searching out Francine's and seizing it.

"Room 1106," he said, a quiver of uncertainty creeping in. "There's a black case under the bed. I think you'd better get it for me, and take care of this—" He handed her the copy of *Variety*, pointing out an employment column on the page, a notice neatly circled. "An appointment I worked myself into it, call and tell 'em I'm running late in traffic."

She looked where his finger was. Smeared black newsprint and an address in Brooklyn.

"The case. Don't forget the case," he said.

"A case of what? What are you smuggling?"

"It's my saxophone," he said, coming as close to a plea as he knew how. "I don't wanna seem intrusive, but you do this, I'm your slave for life. Just go up and get it. I'd do it myself, but—"

Parkins had just hung up, his ear still red from what he had heard, when Boyle began to exhibit the free-swinging style that had made him a lightweight contender. If he went down, he'd go down fighting. "Lookit, my friend," he began, "nothing personal, but since we're both busy men and seeing as how I'm in a special hurry this morning—"

"Being in a special hurry seems to be a trademark of yours, Mr. Boyle," Parkins said, having ample evidence to back him up, if it came to that. "You've run up a nice little bill with us. You've been here almost a week. Where were you before that?"

"Anzio, on the beach. Where were you?"

Even to the armchair onlookers such a claim to heroism sounded awfully tinny, and Parkins wasn't buying it either. He simply flipped over one incriminating document in favor of another and eyed Boyle with heightened suspicion. Boyle didn't exactly stand idle himself. Trying to prod Francine into action, he stepped up the pressure on her open-toed shoes.

It was Parkins' turn to respond. "I'll answer my own questions, Mr. Boyle," he said sharply. "You were at the St. Regis for five nights, three nights at the Gotham, three nights at the Plaza, enjoying room service at each, and in one case use of the hotel limousine. Why do you switch hotels so often, Mr. Boyle?"

It was a provocative question and one Boyle had the quick feet to avoid, instead nudging Francine in the ribs and saying, "I like to listen to the different bands. Eleven hundred and six, all totaled—" He winked. "1106."

She gathered the code was meant for her, but by now she was extremely hesitant to leave. It was starting to get good. There wasn't time for that, though, and she said, "Pardon me," and shoved off.

So convincing was her contempt for him on parting that Boyle was disturbed. He watched her leave and had no idea whether he could count on her to come through. She looked back with a sneer. She certainly looked convincing.

"If you'll follow me, Mr. Boyle," Parkins said without specifying the nature of the threat. "I think it advisable from your point of view."

He held out little hope and opened a small swinging door that would admit Boyle behind the counter, and from there into the office marked "Private." Boyle stalled for time as he watched Francine arrive at the elevators. She gave him the most contemptuous look yet, and she could have fooled him.

"Advisable?" he said, scolding Parkins as he advanced. "One day after V-J Day and you're shaking down vets already. I don't go for that, and neither do my multifarious influential friends at *Collier's* magazine—I got stripes—"

Parkins simply rang a hand bell in front of him, and several bellboys came running, all unnecessarily. Boyle had no intention of fleeing without his saxophone.

"Don't threaten me, Mr. Boyle. Please, this way."

Again he held the little gate open, and a solid citizen stepped through, Johnny Boyle carefully measuring the height of the counter for his return trip.

"Certainly. Anything to clear my name," he said.

Eleven stories up, Francine knocked.

"Open up," she said, looking both ways down the hall. "Francine, house dick."

Eddie DiMuzio opened the door, still fastening his pants. Before he could say a word she was past him. He shut the door, and she went straight for the disordered bed and searched beneath it.

He watched, not minding in the least. He didn't know what she was doing with her head under there, but from this angle he had an inspiration or two.

"Where's Ellen?" she said. With the exception of her strewn underclothes, there wasn't a sign of her.

"She ain't under there," he said. "She's in the john. What're you doing?"

"Five to life, the way it looks," she said, managing to get to her feet with the saxophone case and just now spotting a fatted duffel bag ready for a quick getaway propped next to the door. "The two of you might wanna consider playing house somewhere else. I think your friend's lost the lease. I don't think he believes in paying his bills."

"Who? Johnny?"

"The same." She nodded. "I should have figured he played music. His mouth seems to work all right. Is he any good?"

"Aw, yeah. Sensational," he said as Francine

48

stepped to the bathroom door and listened. "He won all the talent shows, had his own dance band back in Pittsburgh."

"Terrif. Just between us girls, do you mind?"

Eddie stepped aside and she knocked on the door, speaking through it to Ellen. "Alive in there? Any last words?"

No answer, and DiMuzio chimed in. "Too much hooch is all," he said. "The kid's in great shape otherwise. No sweat—I'll take care of her."

"Good luck. I've had her three years on two fronts. She's had every germ known to man. I hope you're different, DiMaggio."

"DiMuzio," he corrected, handing her the copy of *Variety* she was about to leave behind. "This yours?"

"I almost forgot. I think I'm going crazy, with help." She set down the saxophone, the duffel bag, her purse, opened the show-biz bible and reached for the telephone. Looking back later, she would not even remember what she had said but would marvel at her coolness under fire, more importantly the why of it all. Why had she done it? Why had she stuck her neck out when the sensible thing would have been to stay where she was? And she would think of Audie Murphy, other heroes she had read about, who in the moment of battle received a special sort of courage, but who afterward could not tell you why they had done it, or perhaps could not even remember what they had done. War was like that.

She hadn't seen much action in the war, and maybe that was it. She was itching for some combat, but felt robbed by the peace. Oh, she had gotten as far as Papua, had made a mighty threat to the Philippines, had held her ground at Sydney, but then, as luck would have it, she was called back to the States for consultation with her superiors. She was pushing too fast, they said, endangering her supply lines. There were things just as important to be done at home, such as the bond drive. Like a good soldier, she accepted the assignment but didn't like it. She thought of the war, her colleagues at the front, and she itched. Now Boyle was here, and he didn't even read the papers. He was still at war, and the thought occurred to her, they might have some fun together in a last-ditch kind of way.

"Taxi!"

Francine flagged a cab down outside the hotel, threw in Boyle's gear, glancing all the while over her shoulder until she saw him, then waving madly. "Over here!" she yelled.

And Boyle? What was he doing? Pursued by superior forces, he had just run through the revolving door onto the sidewalk, now hesitated a fraction of a second before he saw her, and then made a mad dash for it, Parkins and the bellboys not far behind. When he made the car, he felt cockier than ever, especially once he had the door locked and they couldn't get to him.

"You're in trouble now!" Parkins said, as the taxi started to move and Boyle rolled down his window an inch or two. "Stop this car! I can identify you! I'll notify the authorities—the Army!"

Boyle gave one of his all-time smirks and replied, "Notify your mother! Stick it in your ear, and the horse you rode in on—the war's over."

The last bellboy leaped out of the way, and suddenly the battle was over. An eerie sense of calm pervaded as the taxi accelerated and left the combatants behind, screaming. The victors moved into traffic, smiling at each other. Both in the back seat, they were separated by Johnny's duffel bag, a barrier between them to be overcome.

They rode a minute, each wondering. Johnny didn't know what to say. A "Thank you" wasn't in character. For a while, fortunately only briefly, he considered asking, "What color's Uranus?" He thought better of it and finally said, "So whadda you know—looks like we lost the posse. You want out?"

She shook her head. "It's my cab," she said. "You're welcome to ride."

"Yeah? Where're you headed? Brooklyn?"

"I hadn't decided."

A lot of things had yet to be decided, Boyle thought, looking at his watch and slapping it. It had a habit of stopping like this, like a weak heart, whenever there was a little excitement. He tapped it again. It showed no signs of restarting.

"Anyway, it's nice to know you," he said. "Even my watch don't work. How about that? You electromagnetic or something?"

"Not that I know of."

"You go for science fiction?"

"Not much," she said.

"How about music? You were there last night. You know anything about bands?"

"A little something."

She shouldn't have said that, but how was she to know? With Boyle, you never said you were interested in bands. You always said music bored you stiff. Otherwise it was like giving him an invitation to ruin your day. Pretty soon he would be past the early big bands, advancing in chronological order, and would be up to the birth of bebop, Minton's Playhouse in Harlem, Lester "Prez" Young—President of the Saxophones— Charlie Parker, Jimmy Blanton's bass solos, Charlie Christian's electric guitar, and Jo Jones on high-hat cymbals. All this, if there had been time. Maybe he respected her femininity or what he considered her tender ears. Anyway, this time he skipped it, his two-hour thumbnail sketch of the history of jazz. Instead, he said something remarkable, at least for him, something almost personal, despite his disavowals.

"That creep last night—nothing personal," he said. See what I mean? "But that jerk that cut in on me—"

"He didn't cut in on you. You were through."

"Yeah, well, you know the guy I mean—what's his name? Arnie Trench?"

"That's the name he gave me," she said.

He was looking around the duffel bag in both directions, trying to see her. Finally it was too much, and when something got to be too much for Boyle, he didn't tolerate it. He usually did something.

"I can't see you. I'm gonna move this duffel bag," he said. And he did just that. "Excuse me, buddy," he said to the cabbie and dropped the duffel bag in the front seat beside him, for the first time now being able to look at her and liking what he saw. It was the first time he had seen her in natural light. She looked more natural. And those eyes . . . well, those eyes had a way all their own in the daylight.

"Yeah, Arnie Trench, that's him," he said. "Used to be with Bob Crosby, before that with Sammy Kaye—I started to go up last night and turn his sheet music over for him. I never heard such a travesty of a Sy Oliver arrangement. How could you even be friends with a guy like that, for chrissake, the way he plays?"

She wasn't crazy about the guy herself, but there wasn't any need to tell Boyle that. "What Sy Oliver arrangement?" she said.

"All of 'em. I know 'em all."

She was beginning to get impressed. If he couldn't play, at least he was a helluva fan. "Well, that's a start," she said. "What'd you do, watch him play all night?"

"Yeah, it teed me off. A guy in his position—he oughtta know better."

"I'll be sure and tell him next time I see him. He'll be happy to hear that," she said, smiling at his self-

52

confidence. "If you were in his position, you'd know better. Right?"

"I'd better."

"You've got a pretty inflated idea of yourself, haven't you?"

Boyle mumbled, lit a cigarette. "I haven't got an inflated idea of myself. You're the one that better not get an inflated idea of yourself—that I can't get along without you. Twenty-four hours ago I didn't even know you. You just need to refine your tastes, that's all." About this time he offered her a cigarette, which she declined, and he put the pack back in his pocket. "What'd you say your name was?"

He knew her name, and she knew he knew her name. "I didn't say," she said. "You mean my real name?"

"No, your alias."

"Ida Pizzitola from Boston, Mass."

"But you don't mind if I call you Francine, right?"

"Right," she said.

"That's what I figured."

And his hand crept slowly across the seat, in search of hers, but her hand was still holding the *Variety*. Perhaps unsure what he wanted, he took both.

Chapter 5

THE EXTENT OF JOHNNY'S IMMEDIATE AMBITIONS WAS reflected in the dirty window glass of the destination itself, a Brooklyn dance hall standing in decay and disrepute not far from Myrtle Avenue. The words *Palm Club* were etched on the dark glass and a desert oasis scene painted below, as a taxi pulled up and Johnny Boyle got out.

For a moment he almost closed the door before Francine could swing her legs out, though such was clearly her intention and she let him know in no uncertain terms.

"What are you doing?" she said. "Aren't I coming in? You think I'd miss this?"

And she got out anyway, no thanks to him. "You think I'd miss your audition? Anyway, the guy made a pass at me over the phone. I wanna see what he looks like. You never know, I might decide I like it here—"

She meant that as a joke of course, something to cheer him up, and by now Boyle could use it. How best to say this? But Boyle wasn't his normal self all of a sudden, his normal self-assurance, cockiness even, was nowhere to be seen. He was smoking a cigarette, looking nervous in the sunshine. He even took a couple of tablets out of his pocket and popped them in his mouth.

"If you gotta do something," he said, "go in and tell him I'm here. Tell him I'll be in in a minute."

"What are those?" she said, watching him chew the white tablets.

"Aspirins," he said. "I've got a headache."

That wasn't all. He had a distinct nervous twitch about him, and it was so out of character that she had to ask him about it. First, however, she looked up at the sun overhead to see if the heat might have something to do with it. The sun was hot, but it wasn't that hot, and now Boyle began to play his imaginary saxophone, tooting on an imaginary mouthpiece, putting his fingers on imaginary keys. It was a sight to behold, and he seemed to be playing so hard he began to shiver. She sought a rational explanation.

"What's the matter with you?" she said, trying to snap him out of it. "You're trembling. What are you so scared of?"

At that, he exploded like a coil unleashed, gesturing

54

with his hands and walking in a wide circle. "What the hell you think I'm scared of?" he said, eyes slightly bugging. "I'm scared he'll give me the job and I'll have to play in a place like this. Wouldn't that scare you— to wind up playing your music in a place like this? Spend my whole life here—wouldn't that scare you?"

"You're a young man. What are you talking about?" she said. "How old are you anyway?"

"Twenty-five," he said, fidgeting.

"You've got all the time in the world then," she said, plainly optimistic, trying to cheer up this odd bird she didn't half know. Typical, she thought to herself, getting involved in someone else's life like this. Here she was trying to cheer up this guy she had just met. She didn't know anything about him except that he was acting like a neurotic. Why should she try to cheer him up? Did the world need him? What difference did it make? Why waste her energy? The larger question: Why did she always have to be the one to do everything?

"All the time in the world to do what?" he said, still pacing.

"I don't know. Whatever you wanna do," she said. "How should I know? Why ask me?"

"I'm not asking you."

"Well, if you don't wanna do it, don't do it. That's my advice."

"Don't do what?"

"Whatever you don't wanna do."

He shook his head at that. He wished it could come true, but there were practical considerations. "I need the money," he said. "Just go on in. Tell him I'll be right there."

She looked at him, and that's the way she left him as she went in, still walking in front of the club entrance, puffing a cigarette, playing the unheard song on an invisible saxophone.

Inside, you couldn't see the dance floor for the wax, and you couldn't see the wax for the grime. One of those places. Everything was painted red to conserve fuel.

Shafts of light poured in as the balding club owner raised the blinds and turned to look at Francine, getting it all wrong. What'd you expect? He was still wiping sleep out of his eyes, wasn't in the habit of entertaining well-dressed ladies at this hour of the morning. He had a one-track mind and showed it.

"Hostesses four bits a dance," he recited as if from memory, "but sometimes a dance leads to bigger and better things, if you know what I mean. You turn a trick or two a night, and they don't mind the four bits. Go out in the moonlight, take a walk with the guy. The girls don't do too bad, either. I lose a couple a week to get married—mostly coast guard. We get a lot of coast guard, merchant marine. I got two troubles, musicians and faggots. The faggots play together, but the musicians, never—"

She didn't have to sit still for this and, typically, didn't. She interrupted. "For chrissake, watch your damn language," she said. "Can't you see a lady's present?"

Frankly, he couldn't. He looked at her like she was raising a new and dangerous possibility, and just when it seemed he might reply, she saw something out of the corner of her eye and beat him to the punch, saying, "Anyway, let's get down to business. I'm not the reason I'm here. *He* is."

She meant Johnny Boyle, who had just come in, his eyes taking a moment to adjust in the semidarkness.

"Over here, Johnny," she said, and he came over.

The balding owner was not visibly impressed, watching Boyle approach and forming his own opinion. He had never liked a musician yet, and he saw nothing in Boyle to make him change his mind as Boyle set his case on a table and popped it open. The owner couldn't resist a dig.

"So you're the boy wonder she called about," he said. "You're so good she's gotta do the talking for you."

"I'll do my own goddamn talking," Boyle replied, that strained look about him more violent than anything he actually contemplated, taking a step this way. "Who the hell are you? I don't need this. I don't need to put up with this. I'll step outta this pisshole in a minute—the whole joint smells like piss—"

At which point Francine gently took him aside, even as she smoothed things with the owner. "He's temperamental," she explained, adding within earshot, "Watch your language, Johnny," scolding him like a schoolmarm. Not quite the thing you undertook lightly with Boyle—he was about as receptive to a little friendly advice as Josef Stalin—but, let's face it, she had a way with the guy. Pulling him over by the elbow, she cautioned him with a whisper while keeping an eye on their natural adversary, the pudgy man on the barstool.

"Look," she said, "you're so wonderful, you scare people. Just relax. Let's get the deal straight. If the dough's so good, we don't waste our breath—"

"You're wasting it already," he said. "I don't wanna stay here."

"You got something better in mind?"

"Sure," he said, fibbing. "There must be a hundred places."

"Well, you'd better make up your mind. I'm not gonna sit here and knock my brains out for nothing."

"Sit anywhere you want," he shot back, filling with self-pity at the drop of a hat. "Why don't you sit in his lap? Maybe he'll give you the whole damn club—"

That was uncalled for, and she repaid the snide remark by implanting her high heel on his foot, grinding in retaliation for a number of things. If it did nothing else, the flash of pain cleared Boyle's sinuses and seemed to bring him to his senses as well. Experiencing a possible change of heart, he mumbled something on the order of "Yeah, lookit, I'm sorry. Stick around. I appreciate what you're doing. Sometimes I talk too much, run over at the mouth—and the only cure is putting my foot in it."

He might have said, too, that he was tired of beating his head against the wall, that he'd been looking for employment two weeks without success, that New York's a tough burg when you're down and out, but she knew all that already. She knew what he wanted to say and what he preferred to leave unsaid, too. You might say they began as soul mates from that moment on. Anyway, they certainly presented a united front as they headed back over to the club owner, Johnny trying a new tack.

"What a marvelous complex you got here," he said, whistling as he looked around, taking his sax from his case. The club owner scowled, detecting a hint of sarcasm in Boyle, if his ears heard correctly, just what he'd expect from a wise-ass musician.

"You gonna play or gab all day?" he said.

So the moment of truth arrived, like they were playing the "Macarena" in the background. Could the brash young man from out of town do anything but talk? Could he back it up? Could he play or couldn't he?

Well, if I said he played, you'd say, "So what?" I didn't record it with my secret mike, so you'll have to take my word for it. But, believe me, he played. He played one helluva storm, thrill-packed, if you'd like an adjective, and from the first note he blew, there wasn't any doubt what he knew best in life. It was the first time she'd heard him play, the first time she'd heard anyone play like that, and although she didn't quite understand it, maybe even didn't quite like it, whatever it was, it sent goose bumps up her rump. He was honking and squawking in the lower register like a moaning brat, making Mommy come do what he wanted, making her come to him like he had a Yo-Yo string around his finger. He was shooting notes through the ceiling and making the floor rumble, working complicated riffs that somehow all flowed together in the greater cosmos. If you find this description lacking, I suggest you consult your LP collection. Put on a Sonny Stitt, some of the early stuff. Stitt sounded like Bird, and Boyle sounded like Stitt, so draw your own conclusions. I don't want to be lynched for heresy, but Boyle was that good.

He shut his eyes and blew his cares away. He was always happiest feeling his own vibrations, but it wasn't long before reality intruded in the form of the club owner, who couldn't hear himself think.

"Hey, Boyle," he said, meaning for the young man to keep it down. But Boyle just took a few steps and continued, maybe taking it down a notch but not so you'd notice. If you've never seen a guy play tenor sax in a catatonic state, you've missed one of nature's little wonders.

The owner was getting desperate, and he picked up the first thing he could find. It was a water glass, and he threw it across the room, missing Boyle by a foot or two and finally getting his attention. Boyle lowered his mouthpiece, slowly resuming consciousness.

"Whatever your name is, listen to me," the owner said. "Understand the situation. We got a boy singer here and an eight-piece polka orchestra. Try a little Chevalier. You know any Chevalier?"

"Maurice Chevalier——?" Boyle's hesitation was understandable. It usually preceded a change of color.

"That's right. Some of the boys who come in here

59

just got back from France. They like to hear a little Chevalier, some of those drinking songs—"

"Drinking songs? What're you, nuts?" Boyle said, reverting to normal, seemingly on the verge of tossing aside his saxophone and demanding satisfaction in a primitive way. "Chevalier? That ain't music. What's the matter with you? You look more intelligent—I play that stuff, I kill people—"

The owner drew a sigh. "Yeah? In that case, I'll tell you what. Maybe we're both wasting each other's time—"

But then . . . did I say Chevalier? In a moment when all seemed lost, a third voice entered the picture, the voice of an angel. The heavens had opened to spare Boyle's gig. Just when it looked like the club owner was about to throw up his hands and call the whole thing off, someone started to sing, softly at first but growing louder, singing Chevalier, one of his classics, "You Brought a New Kind of Love to Me"—the same one the Marx Brothers sing in the movie when they're on the boat and trying to fool the customs officials into thinking they're Maurice Chevalier. Each of them tries to pass himself off as Maurice Chevalier, raising a few eyebrows in the process. "Oh, yeah? So you're Maurice Chevalier, are you? Well, let's hear you then!" In the movie it's Harpo who sings like Maurice Chevalier, moving his lips and crooning the words. Unbeknownst to them all, he's got a record player on his back.

She got up on the chair and began to sing fortissimo, wondering even to herself what had gotten into her. But it was doing the trick. Boyle was looking at her again like someone he didn't know but wanted to, seeing something he hadn't seen before, and the club owner lit up a cigar, unabashedly pleased.

Noting the eyes on her, Francine just got more determined and tried to remember the words. She was a pro at this, and she blotted everything else out, especially ignoring Boyle, who was beginning at this late date to take an interest in his own behalf. It was the least he could do, raising his sax and ad-libbing her accompaniment.

"Hey, now, that's more like it," shouted the club owner, enjoying himself, even having a good word to say for Boyle. "Now you're playing something. Can you dance?"

How was Boyle to know? Like an idiot he started to dance while playing the saxophone.

"Not you! Her!" said the owner. "Gimme more, sweetheart!"

He was getting excited, there was no doubt about it. Any minute now he would lean too far forward and fall off his barstool. She started moving her feet, doing a little dance step in the chair, and Johnny blew an impressive riff on his horn. Talents competing, Francine was still the popular choice.

"Let's see the legs, kiddo," the owner shouted hysterically without losing his balance. "Hike your skirt!"

Would she do this? she thought, strange men looking at her. Would she do this? she wondered, and then discovered herself doing it, pulling up the hem of her skirt.

"Hike your skirt, kiddo! That's it. All the way to the garters. I'll make it a boy-girl act, same money I'm paying him—a hundred bucks a week—"

A hundred bucks a week wasn't bad; but here she was, hiking her skirt, practically committing a misdemeanor in a public place. Her head was too muddled to think.

"What?" she said out loud.

And Johnny muttered without skipping a beat, "Just keep dancing."

"That's what my tap teacher used to say," she said, in turn rushing the words without so much as a breath

61

in between. "No matter what happens, no matter what goes wrong, just keep dancing—"

"So keep dancing."

She did and she didn't. She kept dancing, but she didn't tell him why all of this theoretically was impossible. That would have to come later, under the category of life stories and private revelations. Maybe she would tell him tonight. But for the time being, CUT TO MONTAGE.

FILM MONTAGE, their faces, America 1945. Bergman has said that cinema begins with the human face. One minute she's dancing at the Palm Club in an empty room, her arms akimbo, her smile and his conceit, that silly smirk of his surveying all that he's conquered. The next minute they're in a crowded room, and it's her VOICE OVER singing that same Chevalier song over FILE FOOTAGE of famous New York nightspots—neon, neon, and more neon.

They went to the Latin Quarter, for example, where Francine took care of the check. A waiter shook their drinks in a tumbler and a photographer snapped their picture for posterity. From there it was on to the Rainbow Room, the Copacabana, and other choice joints, where Francine picked up the tab. By now it was getting late. At the Copa the waiter lifted a table and carried it overhead for them, as they always did at the Copa.

"Follow me, please."

They had been together since morning, and, what was more, they still liked each other. That was unusual in itself. Both were impatient types and easily bored, but not with each other. Whether they were tired was something else again. They had explored the city, waterfront to seamy side, and now at the end of the long day a slow, weary feeling enveloped them as they rose to dance what had to be easily their fiftieth dance of the night. The music was "Don't Blame Me," and they couldn't resist, hanging close on one another like an extra set of clothes, Francine looking over Johnny's shoulder as he whispered in her ear. His eyes were closed, his feet in shiny Florsheims not exactly gliding.

"Baked beans, Francine Evans and Paul Revere," he mumbled in one man's paradise. "What have these things got in common?"

"Who, me?"

"The Boston Braves, Harvard—Boston, that's where it all began," he said. "Ain't that where you began? An idea somebody had, I had the idea of you."

"Maybe you have the wrong idea," she replied, still looking at something over his shoulder, positioning Johnny anywhere she pleased. "I think you're delirious. You haven't been making sense the last fifteen or twenty minutes. You feel like a duffel bag."

He opened his eyes, noticed she was looking someplace other than into his baby blues, but didn't see what—although we did. She was looking at a guy in the band, that's all. A guy in the band was specifically looking at her, and she couldn't very well not look back. It was obvious they knew each other, like she knew the guy from the Tommy Dorsey band. But Johnny didn't see any of this. As usual, he was off on his own, in his own private mist. The only reason he opened his eyes was to stare disapprovingly at something the saxophones played.

"Yeah?" he said, looking back at her. "I'm a duffel bag? You feel like a sleeping bag."

"That's an insult."

"Well, ain't that how you feel?"

"That's personal," she said.

"Well, stay unzipped. Seriously, Francine, always keep it unzipped for me—"

She looked at him. That was an odd thing for someone to say, an odd way of phrasing it, certainly. But he

63

was perfectly serious, so sincere she felt uncomfortable.

"Let's dance," she said.

She put her chin back on his shoulder and felt him squeeze her closer, if that was possible, their bodies pressing together, and from the bandstand the guy was waving again. The trumpet player. She had always gone for trumpet players before and didn't know why, but now it was time to ask herself. Maybe it was time for a change. But the guy kept waving. What was his name? she asked herself. She was horrible with names and faces, but she never forgot how a guy played. This guy was from Detroit, had been in Krupa's band, but what the hell was his name?

"What's wrong?" Johnny said in her ear.

"Oh, nothing."

And she moved him farther onto the dance floor into the crowd, where they couldn't be seen. She was tired of trumpet players.

Minutes later, the lights of New York filtered into their taxi through raindrops. The radio was playing softly, and the nosy driver tried to overhear their conversation in the back seat, where, despite the setting for romance, what was really going on was a bit of quick-change artistry, one of Boyle's more useful talents. He was changing clothes, civilian for military, assorted garments protruding from the top of his duffel bag, which they had checked earlier with the astonished hatcheck girl at the Latin Quarter. He was halfway through the process, dropping his trousers now as Francine hid her eyes, though peeking through her fingers. She had no idea what he was doing it for.

"Where's my hat, will you—?" he said, scrambling around. "Did you find my hat?"

She found his cloth hat in a pile of clothes and gave it to him. He put it on, and it seemed to fit in with his plans, giving him a more trustworthy appearance.

"Where're you staying tonight?" she said.

64

"I don't know. I figured I'd try the St. Regis."

That was Boyle for you, army trousers and Florsheims, a duffel bag and the St. Regis, meanwhile proceeding with the main topic of conversation. It was life-story time, that part of the movie when man and woman sit back and reminisce about the past, where they've come from, where they want to go in the future, how many kids they'd like to have, the color of the cottage and so forth. "When I was a kid back in South Philly" or "I never will forget what my father told me when I was a kid, after I'd stolen the milk from the milk wagon." But all Boyle had talked about so far was music, and he was up to his twenty-fourth year. He had yet to mention his dear mother or anyone else to whom he owed a great deal.

"You should've seen these jokers down in Texas," he said. "We played half the time with lube oil on our fingers. I had a colored valve-trombone player from Houston. We'd sit up playing jazz all night—you ever play jazz in an aircraft hangar?"

She couldn't say she had.

"We'd play most nights, pass the hat, then go off base weekends and make a few bucks in town. This cat had a sister, nice-looking for a colored girl. . . ." He could have gone on, but something on the radio fortunately intervened. So soft the average human being might not have heard it, Boyle's sensitive ears picked it up immediately, like a prowl dog summoned by high-pitch whistle. He pointed to the radio, telling the driver, "Hey, buddy, turn it up, will you? There's a genius on the radio."

The driver turned it up, and the sound of Benny Goodman filled the car. Benny Goodman playing "Avalon" and Johnny Boyle doing the commentary.

"How's that? The King of Swing—" he said. "You like Goodman?"

She yawned, nodding, putting her head on his shoulder. "Mmm, the greatest of all time," she said.

There was more to it than that, and he let her know. "The greatest of *his* time," he said. "But you gotta remember, it ain't just Goodman. Goodman's three guys rolled into one, all of 'em colored, all of 'em genius in their own right: Fletcher Henderson, Jimmy Mundy and Edgar Sampson—put 'em in the grinder and out comes Benny Goodman's arrangements."

She was convinced he was right and moved closer, slightly upsetting his delicate equilibrium. He looked at her, forced a swallow and continued half-heartedly, "But times have changed. Swing ain't king any more," he was saying, observing how inexorably her lips were coming up to meet his own.

"No? What is king?" she asked, a second before she kissed him, for the sake of her own curiosity.

"I don't know," he said. "Things are looser now, that's all. They're opening up."

"What's opening up?" she whispered in her best throaty voice, sultry and deep, reminding him of Lauren Bacall, her lips hovering, two sets of eyes inches apart in the dark like enemy front lines, and when he didn't have a ready answer, she took the liberty of kissing him again. "Loose?" she said. "You're calling me loose?"

But this time he was set for her, so that when she stepped into his web, he cut off any chance of escape. He wrapped her and squeezed her as if to say, "I'll take it from here," and returned her kiss with something on it.

"You think I'm loose?" she said.

At a moment like this, he wasn't one to judge, and she kissed him once more, this time letting out all the stops. "I'll show you loose," she said, and she certainly did. For a minute the driver up front lost sight of them in his rearview mirror, but it was nothing to be alarmed about. They had only moved deeper into the corner, though his suspicions were heightened when Francine began to moan, murmuring as if in pain. He wondered at the reason for this, as did Boyle himself.

"Let me know if I'm squeezing too hard," Boyle said to her.

"Oh, you're squeezing just fine," she said, taking a breath and biting her lip. "It's my tap shoes. They're murder."

They weren't tap shoes at all, of course. They were just her ordinary shoes. But Boyle came up with a great line. He said, "If they're trying to come between us, throw 'em out the window."

And a minute later, Francine's bare feet stepped from the taxi as if on cue, with a splash in the water at curbside. A few feet away shelter beckoned, but she hesitated and leaned back in the cab to look at Boyle and say goodnight. She was getting drenched. A man from the hotel came over with his black umbrella.

"Johnny, I had a wonderful time," she said. "Don't forget to call me in the morning."

He pulled her in for a kiss, their lips barely grazing before she began to shiver. "Call me, Johnny—I'm getting soaked." And as an afterthought, "Do you have any money?"

"Nothing smaller than a hundred," he said.

"Well, look—" She opened her purse, fumbling, found a couple of ten-dollar bills and started to hand him one. "Take a ten. Stay somewhere decent."

So Boyle did the indecent thing and took both of them, both tens. "For the tip," he said and nudged the cab driver.

"Hey, that's some tip!" she called out.

"I'll call you in the morning."

His smiling face, that remarkable mouth, as he rolled up the window and the cab pulled away from the curb, leaving her under the umbrella, and the rain—

drops, fat and wet—that's the way they said goodbye. Nothing fancy or spectacularly dramatic. Like so much else in life, they planned things one way, and they turned out another. They thought they would see each other again. What was to impede them? They both wanted to, didn't they? Yes . . . so, therefore . . . wherein lay the problem? Francine soon found out.

As she went through the revolving door of her hotel and headed across the lobby, she heard a clerk from the message desk call her name. Turning, she saw him, a wispy little man holding a yellow slip of paper. "Oh, Miss Evans," like they always say so cheerfully in movies of the forties, "message for you."

Trying to dry her hair at the same time, she came over.

"Rotten out there, isn't it?" the man said.

"Yes." She suppressed a slight queasiness as he handed her the paper. A premonition?

"For me?" she said idly, making conversation, unsuspecting. But how would she suspect? After all, it was only the four hundred and fiftieth time in her career for this to happen. The only explanation was that over the course of the day she had suffered temporary amnesia. She had forgotten who she was, what sort of life she led, what she did for a living.

"He said he was your agent," the clerk said. "You a singer or something?"

Maybe she nodded, maybe she didn't. Her heart palpitated, further confirmation. The message was from her agent all right, dear old Tony, a bit of the "welcome back" routine for openers, to pave the way for orders from HQ. She liked the almost jolly way he put it, to ease the shock. "Meet me for a cup of coffee at Pennsylvania Station, 0800 hours. I've got your ticket." Her hand was starting to shake anyway, so she wadded the paper up.

"Of all the miserable—"

"Yes, Miss Evans?" the clerk said.

"No, not you. It's nothing," she said, just stating the facts of life. "It's like everything. You know what I'm saying?"

He just looked at her and smiled politely.

"I mean, you meet a guy you like, and the next thing you know the cotton-pickin' rug is pulled right from under you——" She wasn't getting anywhere with this goony bird. He was still listening but didn't have a clue what she was talking about, though she was beating on the counter to add punctuation. In the space of thirty seconds everything had changed, and she didn't even know why she was wasting her breath. She had no doubt that she would never lay eyes on Johnny Boyle again. She was leaving town in the morning with no forwarding address, and everyone knew Boyle himself lived in a duffel bag.

Her eyes moistening, it was a sudden case of not knowing where to turn. She was on her own and had been for years, granted. This was the kind of thing she had always forewarned herself against, but forewarned is not really forearmed when you encounter Johnny Boyle. And it was considerably more than that, anyway. Boyle was just the tip of the iceberg that sank the *Titanic*. The hollowness in her stomach, the sense of missing something ordinary in life, went way back beyond Boyle, and as she glanced at the lobby full of strangers, people she didn't know, faces she was seeing that she would never see again, a growing feeling of revulsion came over her. She saw them all as another audience, quiet but vicious, expecting her to entertain them or stand on her head if necessary. Faces of monsters in evening wear. God, how she hated this business sometimes. Talk about a tough crowd. When she shook her head, they were gone, but she wasn't. She was still standing at the message desk.

"Are you all right, Miss Evans?" the clerk asked.

She probably reassured him with a word or two and then headed back across the lobby to the front door. She found herself wondering why, even as she did it, but she had to do something. Through the revolving door, she stepped under the awning and signaled the bellman with the umbrella.

"Excuse me, did you see where that taxi went? Did you hear where it was going?" she said.

"What taxi? That one?"

The man pointed at a taxi that was just turning the corner in the next block, its taillights disappearing.

"Yeah, the one that was just here," she said.

He scratched his chin with a large black finger. "That one's going to Pennsylvania Station," he said, then paused. "But the one you want, sugar, plumb done left."

Chapter 6

At 0830 hours later that morning, we're Close on Francine's suitcase, a veritable Pacific almanac of travel decals on scuffed leather—USO, Bob "War Bonds" Hope, Anchorage, Papua, Sydney—effectively announcing a globetrotter and pulling back to reveal:

A bone-weary Francine Evans walking in tandem with a pudgy man alongside a waiting passenger train in Pennsylvania Station the way it looked before they tore it down. Westinghouse brakes frequently interrupted their conversation, but the man with her found ways to speak with his hands. He looked somehow flamboyant despite his lack of physical prowess, a teddy bear with women and a lion among men. He was Tony Harwell, a real sort of movie name. Probably he was Italian or Jewish, or maybe even Greek, from the Mediterranean manner in which he gesticulated whenever she couldn't hear him, in this case because of the public-address system that drowned him out.

"Pennsylvania Central," the P.A. said. "Philadelphia, Washington, now boarding. Last call. All aboard."

Francine seemed not particularly overjoyed by any of it. Her suitcase weighed a ton, and all the travelers around her seemed so happy to be getting aboard that it made it doubly worse. She decided it would be simpler to carry it, and that's what she did, continuing on her way despite Harwell's last-minute offer of assistance.

"Don't walk so fast. Let me take that," he said, meaning the bag.

"Don't hurt yourself. We're almost there," she said. "Anyway, you've got a wife and kids."

She left him holding thin air, and he watched her walk on, now hurrying to catch up. "This ain't peanuts, Evans. I don't know why you're acting like this."

"Like what?"

"The dough ain't bad, and Frankie's a regular guy, you'll see," he said, as they reached her coach. "He'll have a car to meet you."

She took a step up, looked at Tony to say goodbye, when she heard her name, a young soldier calling out from a distance, "Hey, Miss Evans!"

Suddenly it seemed like everyone in New York knew her, and a smile spread over her face. The young soldier in uniform was waving, along with his buddies, and for a fleeting second she thought she saw Johnny Boyle among them. It looked enough like him to be his twin. "Francine Evans!" the same kid kept calling. "Alconbury, England. How's it, for crying out loud?"

Moments like these made it all seem worth it, the train rides, the road maps, the grind. She fired right

71

back at them like the pro she was, wearing a smile. "Great, pal! How's it with you, you ace? Going home?"

"Ain't everybody?" one of the others yelled.

Well, not exactly. Some of us weren't going home. The soldiers trudged on, and she waved after them, one of them walking backward just to look at her. When she finally lowered her arm and turned back to Harwell, her attitude was different, and he sensed it.

"Congratulations," he said.

"For what?"

"For winning the war."

There was nothing to be said, except . . . she remembered and said, "Tony, don't forget. Will you do that for me? The favor?"

He nodded and patted his jacket pocket, the top of a letter protruding.

"Please tell him," she said.

"I'll tell him. Behave yourself."

She couldn't promise to do that, but she threw him a kiss anyway, as the porter hoisted her bag and the train started to move, and she disappeared inside.

Meanwhile, Tony Harwell took several of his duck-like steps beside the train and came to a walking stop below one of the windows, through which a man waved to him. He could see the man and several others in the compartment, and it was evident a party was going on.

"Have a drink?" the man in the window said, offering him a flask.

"No, thanks," he said, and then in response to a general commotion, the man in the window left. There were loud voices and laughter, the unmistakable shriek of a surprised Francine Evans. She came over to the window and hugged the first man, then hugged another, all the time yelling and screaming. Extremely unusual behavior. Had Tony Harwell been an anthropologist instead of an agent, he might have raised his eyebrows. As it was, he knew they all knew each other, and musicians always behaved like that. He watched as long as he was able, until the train was out of sight. Trains always fascinated him. His only regret as an agent was that he couldn't travel more.

Back inside the train compartment, they were breaking out the good booze, and Francine was still squeezing the first man in the window, who happened to be a trumpet player named Paul Wilson. He liked to dress ahead of his time, and just looking at him was a kick for her. Scratch that. The whole thing was a kick.

"I don't believe it!" she said. "I can't believe it! Where's your ticket to?"

"I never heard of it," Paul said.

"That makes two of us. That means we're going the same place," she said excitely, and made him sit down. "That means we'll have time to talk. Paul, I just met the greatest guy in New York—"

Before she could get any more of it out, there was a unanimous groan, the musicians all starting for the door. They had been through this before. Francine's track record with men was legendary. Notice I didn't say good, just legendary.

"Oh, no. Forget it," was their first reaction. "We're not listening to *this!*"

But she was quick to interject, "No, this one's different, I swear. The *least* moves I've ever seen, innocent like a lamb."

Was she talking about Johnny Boyle? Unknown to her, the train headed into a tunnel the minute she said it, a giant phallic symbol. When they came into the light again, she was still talking in a corner with a half-bored Paul, while the other musicians accosted respectable ladies out in the corridor.

"So I said to him, Paul," she said, "Johnny's his name—first you gotta picture the Waldorf. His saxo-

73

phone was upstairs. You remember Ellen Flanery, right? Crazy Ellen? I think you met her."

"I slept with her," he said, looking at the orange New York skyline.

"You slept with everyone. But these days it's not breaking my heart," she said.

He kept looking out the window. Remember her thing for trumpet players? Paul was one of the trumpet players.

"I'm listening," he said.

"Anyway, that's like Ellen's way of shaking hands," she said, getting in a gentle dig. To sleep with Ellen was not like climbing Mount Everest, although in some ways it *was* like that. She was an easy Mount Everest. But she was also Francine's friend, and Francine quickly got back to the original subject. "So, anyway, I was telling you, I go up and get Johnny's saxophone—"

The train rumbled on, Paul already thinking Boyle was totally disgusting, and he hadn't even met the guy yet.

Chapter 7

THAT NIGHT, IN ACCORD WITH FRANCINE'S WISHES, Tony Harwell paid a visit to the Palm Club in Brooklyn. Having made his way past several dance hostesses who admired the cut of his suit, he found the musicians in their customary location, or so he was told, a smoke-filled corner that often smelled sweet. There were half a dozen, half of them black, none of them filling any dire social need. They were just being there, just a lot of chatter and once in a while some music. Nobody noticed Tony Harwell until he made himself known by tapping one of the white fellows on the shoulder.

"Which one of you is Johnny Boyle?" he said.

They all looked at him, and he felt rightly out of place. The corner smelled entirely too sweet.

"Johnny Boyle," he started to say again, and this time he was answered by a blast on the saxophone by the white fellow he had approached to begin with—the youngest of those present, in a porkpie hat, playing the oddest noises. Obviously a fanatic, and from the first Harwell knew there would be a problem with communication. He had given up trying to understand the younger generation, and nothing much they did surprised him any more. Still, all in all, he would have thought Francine had better taste.

"Boyle was here, but he had to leave," Boyle said, suspicious of anyone who addressed him wearing the same fabric from head to foot, whether civilian or military, but it didn't matter by now what he said. Before Boyle even opened his mouth, Harwell was certain he had his man. Francine's description had been right on the money, and he felt actually relieved as Boyle continued, "Boyle's a very busy man, but if you'd like to leave word, I'll make sure he gets it."

Harwell was relieved because he felt in no mood to pass pleasantries. It was much simpler this way, simply reaching into his pocket and handing Boyle the letter. "In that case, just give him this," he said. "He'll understand."

Boyle turned the envelope over, still wary. There was nothing written on it. "Yeah? What if he don't understand?"

To which Harwell called back, for he had already turned to walk away, "Tell him Francine had a wonderful time."

It was like the difference between night and day. At the mention of Francine's name, Boyle abruptly perked up in his chair and took off his hat, desiring suddenly to make a good impression. For all he knew, the fat so-and-so was her rich uncle, and now he was faced with a dilemma requiring some thought. Whether to read the letter or go after the man who had brought it. That morning he had been furious. He had called her hotel, only to be told that she had checked out at seven thirty, mere hours after he had dropped her off and all the mutual promises they had made to see each other again.

Now, as he went in pursuit of Harwell, still carrying his saxophone and trying to read her letter as he went, he got small satisfaction. The letter was mostly polite, nicely written, but . . . polite, full of good manners, "Thank you" and "I'm sorry" and "I really should have told you, but I was having such a good time" . . . things like that. This on the one hand, but that on the other. "Although I find you truly adorable . . ." and "I'm giving this letter to my agent."

So when he caught up with Harwell near the exit, he had a thing or two to say, mostly questions.

"Hey, friend—wait a minute. You legit?"

Boyle had this knack of phrasing things so delicately, like an Oriental at times. Gentle as a rose petal, right? His hand was already on Harwell's shoulder, as the agent turned wearily to confront him, Boyle waving the piece of paper with the slight scent. "Wait a minute, I never seen her writing before. *You* could have wrote this," he said for no readily apparent reason. "I don't believe it."

Harwell could only snort at such a ridiculous suggestion. "Brother, she picks some winners," he said. He could have said a good deal more, but he was anxious to leave. He turned again to do so, but Boyle held him by the elbow.

"You mean she's picked more than one?" Boyle said. "I ain't the first? Listen, I wanna talk to you.

You're her agent, how about being my agent? You must know your way around, right?"

"I found you, didn't I?"

That should have put any thinking person in his place, but Boyle never laid claim to the title. He followed Harwell out of the club to curbside, where Harwell's cab was waiting, an incalculable amount of bullshit meanwhile wafting in the breeze. All Harwell wanted to do was get the hell out of there, but even that would prove difficult.

"For chrissake, whadda they speak where you come from? Don't they speak English?" he shouted at Boyle, thinking he had made it abundantly clear that he wanted to be left alone, which he had. The trouble was with Boyle, who persisted in being friendly with a smirk on his face.

Boyle held the door open for him. "Where're you going now?" he asked. "You going home now to Larchmont?"

Before Harwell could reply, his jaw dropped. Before he could slam the door, Boyle had already gotten into the back seat with him and showed no sign of budging, leaving the normally articulate agent flabbergasted. "What're you doing—? Get out of my—" was all he could manage.

"I just got in New York, see," Boyle said, his saxophone still in his lap. "I've been knocking myself out trying to see the right people, you know, but so far all I'm getting's the brush-off."

"It's hard to figure," Harwell admitted, simultaneously tapping the cab driver. "Let's go."

Surely, he thought, Boyle wouldn't ride with him, but again he didn't know the guy. Boyle rode, and Harwell tried to push him.

"Get out of my—"

But it was no use. Boyle was at the height of his powers and knew it. "It's in her letter," he said, which

77

was so much baloney. "I got permission. Gimme your card!"

"I don't have one."

Harwell wasn't about to give him his business card, but when Boyle responded by blowing a couple of shrill riffs on the saxophone, Harwell reconsidered. The taxi nearly went off the road, and Harwell dug in his pocket. He came up with a card, and Boyle himself urged the cab driver to pull over.

"Pull it over. This is where I get out," he said, taking Harwell's card and looking at him. "I'll call you in the morning. What time do you open?"

Harwell could barely speak, his nerves shattered. "I don't represent lunatics."

Johnny didn't take him seriously. The cab stopped, and he got out, slamming the door hard. Harwell took out a handkerchief and wiped his brow, and as the cab pulled away, he braved a look at Johnny standing on the corner, regarding him as he would a spaceman.

My God, he said to himself and returned his handkerchief to his pocket. He wasn't used to this, and he thought he'd seen it all.

MUSIC DOWN, low and blue. This is the part of the movie where the hero stands on a lonely street corner in the night air and smiles to himself, his cares far away. Now it was Boyle's turn. The Palm Club was a block away, but seemed miles. He had come this far in a matter of minutes, but had much farther to go. He studied Harwell's card with obvious satisfaction, like a lock of hair lopped off in battle, then sat down on the curb and began to play the saxophone as the spirit moved him. In a while the spirit moved him to play "Once in a While," a timely tune whose lyrics soon could be heard remarkably well, Francine's crystal VOICE COMING UP in background.

THE
BAND

Chapter 1

HERE FOLLOWS OUR FIRST GLIMPSE OF FRANCINE Evans the performer, standing at the mike in front of the Frankie Clarke band, somewhere on the road, performing "Once in a While," then "I'm Sitting on Top of the World" at different mikes in different locales, singing for different audiences in different dresses, at times even dressing like the boys in the band in the Anita O'Day style ... riding the bus with the Frankie Clarke logo on the side, the bus moving past road signs and varied landscape, the names of locales passing rapidly, Richmond, Roanoke, Scranton, etcetera.

At one point the bus stops at a railroad crossing, and our attention turns to a train that goes smoking by. CLOSE SHOT on one of the train windows, Johnny Boyle's face looking back at the bus. Their paths have accidentally crisscrossed, defying impossible odds.

Finally we spy Johnny in a telephone booth somewhere in a small-town railroad station, barking into the phone, trying to make himself heard, looking over his shoulder at the same time, the waiting passenger train about to leave without him.

"Hello? Where?" Johnny says into the phone. "This is Covington, Virginia. Is this Virginia Beach? Is the Frankie Clarke band there? They've gone where? How do you spell that? What state's that?"

The waiting train waits no longer, sounds its whistle, and starts to pull away, as Johnny hangs up, grabs his bag, and pursues, catching up to the train, holding on to his hat, and jumping aboard.

On the bandstand the Frankie Clarke band, overlooking a large and mostly empty ballroom, even spooky, but elegant ... Frankie Clarke himself at the microphone and taking an inordinate amount of time fussing with its height, using the opportunity to gauge the evening's attendance, spotty at best, as Francine stepped up to sing in a shimmering dress.

The front of The Greenbrier hotel, a stately white resort ... grandeur of another day ... high Colonial columns, as Boyle ENTERS FRAME, his back to us, shoes treading through fallen leaves, heading up winding sidewalk.

In the foyer outside the ballroom, he handed his hat to a hatcheck girl, glancing at a nearby sign on an easel that bore a glossy eight-by-ten photograph of Frankie Clarke under the caption *Now Appearing at The Greenbrier, with His Orchestra*—a very old-fashioned advertisement in the first place. Frankie Clarke was a middle-aged man with a mustache who had been around practically forever, meaning in the business, and in the next room Boyle could hear the band playing a traditional ballad in the time-honored way, Francine doing the honors on "I Had the Craziest Dream." It was as though music had stood still in this place for the past ten years, kept in these splendid surroundings like a slightly moldy stuffed pheasant. White Sulphur Springs loved Hal Kemp arrangements, but they must not have loved them too much, or they wouldn't have stayed away in such droves. Boyle will go down in history a singularly unimpressed. The band had a lousy sound. Surely it wasn't that they were incapable of playing better, he reasoned, which must mean that they were playing for the purists who were nowhere to be seen.

"Will you sign, please, sir?" the hatcheck girl said, presenting him with the book. She was quite pretty in a plantation sort of way, but Boyle's geography was a little off. West Virginia had seceded from the South at the start of the Civil War, and she turned out to be a coal-miner's daughter. Boyle learned all this as he signed the book and commented on the picture of Frankie Clarke on the poster marquee.

"Look at that," he said, using a particularly expansive gesture. "Who wants to look at that? They oughtta have a pretty puss on there, like yours, for instance—"

"You an expert or something?" she said.

"Yeah, an expert on pusses. I'm a friend of the band."

He smiled, and she had one to top that. "They need all the friends they can get," she said.

There were possibilities that glimmered in her eyes, and pure larceny in his. By the time he left he had her phone number. He was still shaking his head over Frankie's ugly picture as he finally headed inside.

"See you around. What's your name—Miss Hat?"

"Louise."

Francine was still at the mike, singing "I'm Confessing My Love." As she sang, she was looking out across a vast wasteland of shiny waxed dance floor, mostly uninhabited, ceiling decorations ostentatious in their loneliness, hotel guests seated here and there at scattered tables—and way at the rear of the enormous hall she spotted a solitary figure coming in.

The two of them regarded one another after weeks apart, first from Johnny's lingering point of view at the back and now as he came forward, from hers at the mike as she sang the song through to conclusion; and Johnny began to clap as he advanced, getting the attention of almost everyone, applauding politely as he strode across the swank salon.

He was actually applauding for everybody, applauding for her, applauding the dancers, applauding for himself and the architecture—anything to get a little notice, finally reaching a desired seat, and still applauding as he sat—nothing loud, just loud enough to strike a nerve, putting his palms together lightly, moving his head around, looking at everything, just indulging the urge.

The effect of this insolent behavior—and some of it was that—was to arouse great indignation among the musicians, as Francine learned to her dismay. She could see Boyle as the new boy, already getting off on the wrong foot, and before he did something else to get himself in deeper, she turned from the mike and looked to Frankie Clarke at the keyboard, pinning her hopes on him. He was taking a drink of water, poised to lead the band into its next ever-popular requested number.

"Frankie, you need me for a couple of minutes?" she said. "I think I need to collect myself."

Frankie gulped, set down his water, and looked in the direction of Boyle's table, where by now Boyle had become the center of attention among other patrons around him—he was applauding them, and they were applauding him, like that.

"They oughtta collect that guy," he muttered. "He keeps clapping, I'm going over there myself, stuff that clown in the garbage."

"I go for clowns, Frankie," she said. "I'll do it."

Frankie didn't say yes and he didn't say no. He just watched as she left the bandstand and he cued up the band for the next spot, entitled "Give Me the Simple Life." And how, brother. And how. If business didn't pick up, he would as soon be on his farm in Florida, watching his orchards freeze. He'd been at it too long to take this kind of abuse. He was rapidly losing his enthusiasm for great music.

As the band played anyway, Francine approached Johnny's seat, the tables around him having become a cluster unto themselves, well-heeled tourists laughing and clapping, the atmosphere of an ocean voyage. Friendly introductions were in progress, as Johnny, the life of the party, shook hands across tables, on his feet as Francine arrived. He was having such a good time, very little could change his mind.

"My, my, New York, wasn't it?" she said, her face slightly flushed, with one eye on the band. "Excuse me, but you've caused me considerable personal embarrassment, and I think they're signaling you. Your flat's fixed."

"What flat? Francine, get a load of these characters—they're all in the movies."

"You're the one who's flat, sister," said a drunken tycoon with a pale wife, provoking Boyle's ire.

"You wanna see flat?" Boyle said to him. "I'll put you over my knee and slap your face."

That got a laugh, as did Boyle's false step in the man's direction, at the same time feeling someone's hard grip on his elbow and a voice in his ear.

"Sit down and shut up," Paul Wilson said.

He had come over from the bandstand, thinking Francine might be in need of help, his masculine sense of self now enhanced as he pushed Boyle into a chair.

But Boyle bounds to his feet, and we know what to expect.

"Paul, don't," Francine implored. "He's a vet. I can manage—I did it in the war."

Boyle was still glaring at Paul, both ready to charge on command. "Who? Me?" Boyle snarled.

"Yeah, you. This is a classy joint. Sit down and listen to the music or get out."

"What music? Where?" Boyle is wondering aloud, taking a half-step closer, Francine bracing herself for possible intervention.

"Paul, please," she said. "Oh, God—this is Johnny, the guy that—"

Naturally, Paul misunderstood, thinking instead of someone else and getting even angrier. "This is the guy that—?"

"No, not that guy," she moaned. "This is another one."

One was bad enough.

"This is another one?" he demanded.

Paul was rolling up his sleeves, and Boyle was feeling left out, simply looking on. "You talking to me? Who's talking to me?"

"No one," Francine said. "Go outside."

She pushed him on his way, Johnny insisting on looking back at Paul, both equally reluctant to give up their potshots at one another. "I just wanna talk to the young lady," Boyle said, throwing the challenge. "What's it to you?"

"You're bothering her," Paul said.

"Yeah? C'mere, I'll bother you."

That juvenile boast, followed closely by another brief outburst of handclapping, was enough to send Paul off his rocker. He made a fearsome lunge for Johnny and came close enough to knock several drinks off a table and tear a button off Johnny's jacket, before Francine pushed him back and took Johnny in tow with all the authority of a drill sergeant, pausing only to pick up spilled wineglasses in her path.

She put the glasses back on the table, explaining as best she could to the patrons who had had to witness the entire shameful spectacle. "Business is slow. We're all a little edgy," she confided nervously. "Bring your friends next time."

At that, they gave her a surprising round of applause, and she and Johnny went out together, as through it all the band played on . . . now striking up with its version of "I'll Get By," one of the major existentialist songs in its repertoire.

85

Chapter 2

WHAT THEY DISCUSSED THAT FIRST TIME OUT WAS anybody's guess, but later, after the show, two pairs of feet walked through the autumn leaves that swept across the sidewalk in the moonlight, and Francine and Johnny could be heard arguing in low voices, heads down, strolling in step, appearing as rather ghostly figures from a distance across the lawn.

Johnny was wearing his best suit with a button now missing, Francine a white coat thrown over her long dress ... the two of them resembling more than anything refugees from the Junior Prom ... now separating against the backdrop of The Greenbrier, moving apart to come back together farther up the sidewalk, Johnny yelling after her white silhouette as she walked away.

"Something!" he said. "You could have told me—something! You're calling me names, I got one for you—the Phantom of New York. Whadda you think of that? How do you think I felt when I read that letter? Speaking of good manners, how about telling the truth when you're with a person? Ain't that good etiquette any more?"

"Not always," she said, walking, kicking the leaves. "I got one for you, but you wouldn't understand it. How do you think I felt? You think I enjoyed keeping you in the dark? But what would I have told you? Next year in Jerusalem? Next V-J Day in New York? Mark your calendar? This is it, this is what I do. I meet people in a hurry, I say goodbye through windows—"

"So I heard. Not to me, you don't." Boyle had a habit of punching the air with his finger, an old debating technique. "You don't tell me goodbye, sweetheart—I tell you goodbye!"

Now she was angered as well, her lower lip slightly puckered and jutting. "So that's what's bothering you—so tell me. Get it off your chest. That's what's really bothering you most of all, that any woman in her right mind could tell you goodbye or, what's worse, could leave without telling you anything. Well, I admit it, I'm not in my right mind, if it makes you feel any better. Any sane girl would have dropped everything in her life to stay in New York with you and get arrested."

Now Boyle was backing off, and she was just getting going, her temper slower to burn. "So get it off your chest," she said. "Tell me 'So long, sweetie,' with your best 'So long,' and you'll feel better and you can go home. You'll feel like a man. Go on."

He just looked at her, blinking. "I just got here," he said. "Don't rush me. I ain't decided yet. Maybe I'll stick around, see about the situation—"

"What situation? What're you trying to say?"

"Don't laugh. I'm talking about the band," he said—a thought that had already crossed her mind. "I'm considering the possibilities."

"What possibilities? You? You come here, no plan, no strategy, no road map—you get in a fight and you don't even know what state you're in. What kind of possibilities is that?"

"I got a plan," he retorted, punching the night air. "It's a state you don't know. C'mere and feel what state I'm in. You're so smart."

She *was* so smart. The idea of seeing him again had occurred to her frequently, but she would never have taken the initiative, even had she known how to go about it. It wasn't the most promising of circumstances for a budding relationship, three hundred one-nighters a year, and if it wasn't three hundred, it felt like four

87

hundred. She would never have encouraged him, but now that he was here . . . What made sense? Put him back on the train, send him back where he came from, stash him under her bed, sneak him onto the tour? You're right, none of it made sense. So now there was a moment of reconciliation in the chill of the night while both looked at one another and considered the future with and without the other, the fight seemingly going out of them, until Boyle had to pipe up and add resentfully, "You're so smart you don't even realize what I meant when I told you to keep it unzipped for me."

"Oh. I see—keeping it unzipped for you means that you care. Isn't that a little cryptic?"

"I'm not cryptic—I'm Irish."

"Don't you know what 'cryptic' is?"

Boyle had gone to high school. "Sure, cryptics are Catholics living in Egypt."

She laughed. "Ha! Those aren't cryptics—they're Coptics!"

She had him now, but before she could gloat, he said, "Don't change the subject. I love you."

Words were caught in her throat, and suddenly both of them stopped the foolishness. The horseplay, if not the foreplay, was over, and they came together for a kiss, Francine borrowing her lips for a moment to say, "A casual love—is this a casual love, Johnny? I always wanted a casual love."

Even she probably didn't know what she meant by that. She had always had a poetic bent, and it sounded poetic. She wrote poems herself and would doubtlessly write one about this, capturing this instant for immortality like Elizabeth Browning. A great love of the century, a famous scandalous dalliance—she had dreams of both. "Or the time of roses, from Swinburne?" she said. "When you drink, do you eat the lemon rind?"

Lately she had felt an inexplicable attraction toward

men who consumed their lemon rinds whole when they drank. She didn't know what it meant, and in fact had seen no one do it, but she knew if anyone did, it would be Johnny Boyle. She took a step away from him accordingly and executed an unlikely minuet step under the sky full of stars, slowly turning in her white coat until he pulled her next to him and pressed her close.

"Be quiet," he whispered, looking in her eyes. "You ever try to catch a band without a scorecard? The original bloodhound, I missed you by an hour in Scranton, two weeks in the Poconos, ten minutes in Reading, and I swore I'd make it up to you."

"I'll take two weeks in the Poconos."

He kissed her. "You'll take ten minutes in Reading and like it," he said.

She liked it when he stuck out his chin so assertively and gave the illusion of knowing what he was doing, although actually he was just leaving himself open for a good left hook.

"No one's arguing," she said.

Chapter 3

AN HOUR LATER IN THE DESERTED GREENBRIER BALL-room, Johnny Boyle blowing great saxophone, flights of fantasy, none of it on paper . . . bebop obbligatos and the changing times, as he stood on the bandstand alone, although soon there were witnesses. Members of the band began to stick their heads in the door, some intoxicated, some half asleep, but all knowing a good sound when they heard it—not the least of whom was Frankie Clarke.

At Francine's instigation, Frankie now crossed the room, Boyle momentarily stopping to get a breath but too insecure not to keep playing. He started howling again through the sax, music Frankie was hard pressed to identify, much less identify with. At least on the surface, it would seem the two of them had little in common. Boyle's music certainly wasn't the sort of thing the band played, and for a few seconds Frankie just stared at him. Then, without saying a word, he gave a silent nod of approval and sat down at the piano to plunk out a lively accompaniment, and the duet began. As they played, Frankie gave subsequent little signals, almost imperceptible to the naked eye, and Boyle toned it down for the sake of decorum, proving he could play like the rest of the band, and also because guests in the rooms above were beginning to complain of strange vibrations even when the Niagara was off.

So, with a little help from his friends, Boyle was hired, and he was as mystified as anyone. No one could figure the odd affinity Frankie Clarke seemed to feel for him, unless it was a matter of the middle-aged artist seeing himself as a young man, perhaps envying some quality of Boyle's—his youth, his freshness. Maybe there was a bold daring in Frankie's makeup struggling to break forth to fruition after all this time, and then again, maybe there wasn't. But whatever the reason, when the bus pulled out of town a few mornings later, Boyle was on it, riding the broken white line with the rest of them, wheels turning underfoot and his head spinning. Boyle was so happy he even called his mother and told her he had survived the war. He thought he had found his niche.

At least part of that niche involved riding next to Francine, the two of them curled up under a blanket in their customary spot in the back of the bus. While those around them flaked out in that semiconscious state of highway travel or played cards, Boyle usually blew the saxophone, as loud as they would let him get away with. One evening, somewhere in Ohio, he blew a

90

melody Francine hadn't heard before, and since she was under the impression she had heard every tune he knew several times, she stirred in her slumber.

"Whadda you call that?" she said.

Johnny was blowing his horn down low, a bebop sound, and that's what he thought she meant.

"It's a honk," he said. "Just honks under the melody."

But it was precisely the melody that interested her. "What melody?" she said.

"This, it goes like this—"

And he proceeded to play it again, honking and squawking madly, though missing the point as far as she was concerned. It was a very pretty melody.

"What is it?" she asked again, going on the assumption that if you asked Boyle a simple question three times, you had a chance of getting through.

"Nah, it's nothing, just a little piece. After this, I go over here to this—" And he showed her on a piece of sheet music propped up on his knee, propped up in turn on the seat in front. But he still wasn't answering her, and when he started to play again, she clamped her fingers over his keys to stop him.

"No, I mean the melody—the whole song. What's it called? I never heard it before."

"It never *was* before." He shrugged. "I don't know, it's nothing. Just something I was fooling around with one night in New York."

"Someone or something?" she inquired judiciously.

"It's just a song, that's all—something I wrote. Why, what's the matter with it?"

"Nothing's the matter with it. You really wrote it?" she said, honestly impressed. "Hey, that's terrific. It's a terrific song."

"Knock it off," he said, convinced she had to be pulling his leg, but she was in dead earnest. She took the sheet music off his lap and looked it over.

"You need some words," she said.

"What words? Forget it."

"Well, you've gotta call it something. We need at least a title."

"Whadda you mean 'we'?" he said.

One of her better dirty looks changed his mind.

"I'm waiting for an inspiration," he said. "How about 'December the Seventh'?"

"Pearl Harbor?"

"Today's December the seventh."

"No."

Just no. That wouldn't do. She had adopted the song and would give it a name herself, as well as write the lyrics. She, too, was waiting for an inspiration, when he said, "Let's name it after where we are. Where the hell are we?"

As luck would have it, they were traveling through a darkened town as she looked out the window.

"Yellowbud, Ohio," she announced, then paused, having second thoughts. "I don't know, it doesn't quite have that ring to it, you know?"

"What's wrong with 'Yellow Butt'?" he said. "Sounds OK."

"Well, it's not very romantic. Why don't we name it after where we were, instead?"

"Beaver Falls?"

That was night before last.

"No, New York. 'New York, New York,' " she said.

He had no objections. "Wish I'd thought of that," he said.

Down near the front, they were trying to play cards, Paul Wilson, Frankie Clarke and a couple of others. They had no respect for Boyle because he never played. He didn't know an ace from a club and was therefore considered slightly abnormal. He didn't talk baseball, knew next to nothing about sports, didn't know a double-play combo from a dime in the

92

jukebox. All he knew was that goddamn horn, and now he persisted in playing it through their card game.

"Hey, Beethoven," Paul Wilson finally shouted back at him. "Money riding up here, will you—ease off? People trying to sleep."

The sax went down but not out, Boyle lowering the volume to a murmur, and Paul flipped a card, looking disgusted. He couldn't blame his luck on Boyle and didn't try, for contrary to his public attitude, he had lately been forced to reassess his initial opinion of Boyle and had reached a startling conclusion. "You heard much of Boyle's stuff, Frankie?" he asked Frankie Clarke across the makeshift table. "He's a heck of an arranger. He really knows what he's doing."

"I never had any doubts of that," Frankie said, his look obviously concealing more than he chose to tell, as he swept the winner's chips into his corner. If only life were this simple. "I oughtta be doing this full time," he argued. "Change my line of work—the odds are better. Nicky, get me a Bromo, will you?"

"Why? You want me to tell your fortune?" Nicky said.

"Yeah."

Nicky, the drummer, got up to get the Bromo, having lately taken to telling Frankie's fortune in the way it fizzed, each bubble something different.

Chapter 4

OF COURSE IT WASN'T ALL ROSES FOR BOYLE. A PER-sonality like his, sooner or later he had to run into rough spots, like the night he stood up to play his first solo. Oh, it was great, a great bit of virtuosity, and don't let anyone tell you Boyle didn't love performing.

He didn't like the headaches, but he loved the spotlight, and that night he was untouchable, playing a particularly good spot, and when he sat down, the fellow next to him on alto—whose name now eludes me—leaned over and gave him a begrudging nod.

"Nice spot," the fellow said.

"You said it," Boyle said. "Now get a load of this one."

And saying that, he took everyone by surprise and stood up again. To say "surprise" was even understating it. Frankie almost went into shock. Here was this idiot in the back row getting to his feet for an encore and going right into another solo that no one had counted on, doing it only because he had liked the thrill of the first one so much he had decided to try another. The rest of the guys had no choice but to stop whatever they were doing and listen to him again. Needless to say, such behavior rankled, and from the looks on the faces of those around him, Boyle hadn't heard the last of it.

They were waiting for him afterward. They, Paul Wilson, among others, cornered him in a fistfight after the show, with the intention of settling the score, but it wasn't as serious as it sounds. Boyle had no cause to worry. If you've ever seen musicians fight, you know where the concept of shadowboxing originated. Lest anyone get hurt and endanger his livelihood, musicians fight by throwing punches to the shoulder. So when the guys invited Boyle to step around the corner and join them in a little war council, he went willingly enough, telling Francine he'd be right back.

"If I'm not back in ten minutes, call the police," he told her in parting.

But when ten minutes passed without word of him and a drizzle began to fall, she went to find him. She appreciated a good prank as much as the next fellow, but one could take things too far. Sure, Johnny had made an ass of himself by standing up for a second solo, but you could put it down to rookie inexperience, and as a rookie, he worried her.

When she turned the corner, she saw her fears were groundless. Oh, they were swinging at him all right. They were all tearing into him, but no one was swinging at any vital points. In fact, Paul Wilson was shouting as a reminder, "Watch his lip!"

Maybe there was an accident, or maybe Boyle was just putting on a performance, but he started yelling, "He hit my lip! He hit my lip!"

But there was no sign of any damage, just a lot of shoving. Tempers were still flaring, though, and one of the guys grabbed Boyle in a full nelson while Boyle pushed another to the pavement, still protesting, "My chops! He got me in the chops!"

"What's the idea, Boyle?" Wilson said. "Trying to make us look bad tonight? You're showing us up, Boyle."

Boyle pushed off, throwing Paul against a garbage can, gripping him by the shirt collar. "Just don't hit me in the chops, or I'll bust you in the fucking mouth. As for making you look bad, your mother ain't here to defend you, so leave her out of it—"

It went on that way, more scuffling, until Francine decided to break it up. It wasn't difficult. "That's all! Stop it!" she said.

They were all just waiting for an excuse anyway.

"What the hell took you so long?" Boyle grumbled, rearranging his clothes.

They had all turned to look at her, making occasional grabs for one another, but nothing that couldn't be held in check, and she positioned herself strategically, reacting firmly when Paul gave Boyle one last push.

"That's enough, Paul! I won't have it—leave him alone."

"You're taking his side," Paul said, the others concurring. It was predictable.

"I'm not taking his side," she said. "He got what was coming to him. Look at him, he's a bloody pulp."

There wasn't a mark on him, nothing that a trip to the cleaners couldn't iron out. Even so, Boyle was pouting, feeling very much the martyred Saint Bop.

"You saw what he pulled tonight," Paul said. "Trying to show us up—"

"I *did* show you up," Boyle interjected, inciting Paul again.

"See there—he admits it!" Paul said, and the two of them were at it again, exchanging harmless punches until Francine physically separated them.

"You heard him!" Paul continued.

"Watch it!" she said.

It was Boyle's turn. "Yeah? Whadda you call that crap we play every night—music?"

"I call it crap," Paul agreed.

"Ha!" Boyle said, thinking his point was made, but unnerved that Paul agreed with him. He made a mental note to reassess Paul Wilson, but then Paul added, "Nothing wrong with playing crap. That's why we got a singer."

And now suddenly it was Francine who took exception, turning on Paul with a fierceness that took even Boyle by surprise. "Hey, speak for yourself!" she said. "I don't think it's fair—"

Now it was Boyle holding back Francine, who was straining to get at Paul. "Easy, Francine—cool it!"

What cooled it was a cloudburst; the rain started to come down harder, as Paul retreated with apologies to all.

"Take it back!" she demanded.

"I didn't mean it like that," he said, raising his voice. "Nothing about you. This band ain't going nowhere, that's all. Boyle's right."

"No, he ain't right," she said, putting her foot down, bringing the two factions together. "We *are* going someplace. All we gotta do is stick together. We're all going for a drink, and I'm buying. C'mon, it's pouring down."

Both of them caught cold from that little experience, standing too long out in the rain with their dukes up, but when things are going your way, even a case of the sniffles has its advantages. One must stay in bed and keep warm, and neither of them had any trouble with doctor's orders. Sometimes they cuddled in her bed and sometimes in his, though for appearances' sake, they always slept apart. That is, until one night in Boyle's cubicle, which proved exceptionally cold. It must have been a blizzard out of the north, meaning the Great Lakes. They were in Bloomington—"ensconced," as Boyle would say—and for some mysterious reason he had neglected to shut his window, which would explain the snow particles flying freely through the room. The wind was whipping the curtains, and her teeth were chattering.

"Who started this?" she whispered, pulling the covers up snug to her chin.

"Who—what?"

"Doing it in the raw." Raw was right; she was freezing.

"It goes back," he said. "The Pharoahs."

"Yes, but it's hot over there. Johnny, shut the window, please. You win, I'll stay all night. It's too cold to leave."

That seemed to satisfy him, and he reached up to loosen a length of cord that was ingeniously attached

97

to the wall through a system of pulleys, so that with a flick of the wrist he could raise and lower the window at will. When he lowered it, the snowflakes slowly settled around their feet.

"Nice to see you stay," he said. "Happy to accommodate you."

"Happy to have been accommodated."

She kissed him, the kiss serving to distract him from her hand, which was slipping under the sheet for purposes of exploration. "As Johnson said to Boswell," she said, expecting him to think of something clever, although she didn't know why. He never did.

"Aw, keep it under your hat," he said.

By now her hand was below his navel and groping. "I'd like to," she replied. "If I had a bigger hat."

She held him, and he got bigger. They shared a kiss, and it was morning before they knew it. The first thing Johnny Boyle saw when he opened his eyes was the sun shining on Francine's shoulders as she sat at the desk and scribbled something in the small spiral notebook she always carried with her. He had tried to sneak peeks at various times but had never succeeded in seeing what she wrote. But that was soon to change. She didn't see him sneak out of bed and come over, didn't feel him until he put his hands on her and looked over her shoulder.

"C'mon, lemme see," he said as she tried to put a hand over the page. "You never show me what you write."

"I'm embarrassed," she said.

He took the book anyway and read, his eyes getting moist for the second time in his life. God, how he loved her. There were nothing but poems here, pages of them, poems and lyrics and more poems, some of it pretty avant-garde stuff. I mean, what did Boyle know from poetry? But he knew what he liked, and here's one that caught his eye, written only this morning.

SONG BIRD

Love is like the song bird
Who sings in a strong voice
Night and day
And of dying knows nothing
Until the hour of its death
When its song ends
And from the sky
It falls.

Or this short one on the page before:

SEA GULL

Dead gull, lying on the sand
But who can look at you
Without remembering
That only yesterday
He admired your flight.

Or the one before that, entitled "Skylark":

SKYLARK

Skylark, your life is flying
Over the rivers and to the sea
And if one day your wings endure
You'll reach heaven, surely,
Or even come to me.

She liked birds, and there wasn't a dry eye in the house when Boyle mumbled through one aloud, one entitled "The Pelican."

"You wrote this?" he said.

She nodded.

"They're poems," he said. "They're terrific, especially this one. I'm all this? I'm 'The Pelican'?"

She assured him he was, and he gave her a caress,

which was all he could manage. His mood had changed, as he quickly moved to the bathroom and shut the door, leaving her alone for several seconds. She had no inkling as to what he was up to. There was no sound from behind the door, but when he emerged, it was clear he had been in conference with himself. The decision reached was final.

"I'm getting tired of this," he said. "Get your clothes on. We can't go on like this."

"Go on like what? Johnny—"

She had no idea what he was talking about, and he didn't give her time to ask questions, tossing her her bra, doubtless meaning business.

"You heard me. We can't keep meeting like this. I'm calling a cab."

"Where're we going?"

"You'll find out."

An hour later they walked into a rustic lodge thirty miles outside of town and confronted a kindly old justice of the peace with a badge on his chest. In the best Hollywood tradition, it was one of those classic log-cabin honeymoon hideaways, complete with the elk's head over the check-in desk, and the concerned frown of the crusty old J.P., looking dismayed to see his young lovers apparently having a spat as they came through the front door.

"Do you have reservations?" he asked them.

"A few, but we're staying here anyway," Francine said, borrowing a line from vaudeville, and if it wasn't from vaudeville, it should have been.

"We want the honeymoon special," Boyle blurted out, hoping to put an end to the squabbling, but Francine wasn't so easily mollified. Something had stuck in her craw, and she wasn't going to let him off the hook until she got satisfaction.

"Of all the unbelievable—" she said to him, stammering in her incredulity. "That was it, wasn't it? The whole thing. That was the best you could do?"

"What?" he said, pleading innocence.

"Your proposal, if that's what you wanna call it. That was all of it."

Boyle didn't like the look the old man was giving him and all that it implied. Officially the old geezer represented the law hereabouts and obviously sided with Francine in the argument, though he was out of earshot. Boyle decided the moment called for bold action, and taking Francine by the arm, he said, "Why? You want me to do it again? Come on."

He walked her by the elbow back outside again, despite her protests and those of the J.P., who pleaded for a reconciliation.

"Children," he said.

"Johnny, you can't do it again. This is ridiculous."

It was ridiculous, but outside he led her back down the snowy walk to where their cab was still waiting, the cause for all the commotion his initial proposal, one she evidently believed fell short of the mark.

"I'll show you," he said, leading the way, his jaw firm.

"You can't do it again. You already did it."

"That was rehearsal."

"You can't do it again."

She had never heard of anyone proposing twice. It just wouldn't be the same. He'd had his chance already.

But try to tell him that. "Of course I can do it again," he said. "You watch—brace yourself. Just sit tight."

He pushed her back into the taxi and slammed the door, heading back around to his side of the car, feeling his masculinity insulted. The justice of the peace had meanwhile come out to the front porch, as

Johnny mumbled to himself, shot a fresh look of determination at the old man, and opened his door.

"I'll do the best goddamn proposal you ever saw," he said, vowing to wow 'em as he got back in the car. "Get a load of this one."

ANOTHER ANGLE, as he took her in his arms in true Valentino style, the windows of the back seat fogging, and APPLAUSE carried over from the following scene ... the guys in the band applauding from the windows of the bus the next morning, as Johnny and Francine emerge bleary-eyed from their cabin at the honeymoon courts. ... MORE MONTAGE, wheels of the bus, and the open road ... another town, another show ... another poster going up, *Frankie Clarke and His Orchestra*, another sad hotel.

Chapter 5

FRANKIE CLARKE LOOKED AT THE CALENDAR. He didn't even know what day it was. When he knew what day it was, he knew what town he was in.

He was sitting in his cluttered hotel room amid room service coffee cups, still wearing his pajamas, and it was three in the afternoon. At his side were a couple of fellows in shirt-sleeves and sun visors, obviously bookkeepers, judging by the color of their suspenders—red, to match the red ink that seemed the chief subject under discussion here, indeed the reason they have all come together, to hunch like Zurich gnomes over the band's woeful ledgers.

It looked like bad news, and there was more on the way, as someone knocked at the door and Frankie looked up, irritated and yet relieved to be interrupted at such an unpleasant task.

"Who is it?"

Without waiting to be invited, Boyle opened the door and came in. He and Frankie had been on pretty good terms lately, but that was on days when Frankie could put himself in the mood for it, and today was another story.

"You busy, Frankie? It's me."

"I know it's you, Boyle. Whadda you want?"

Boyle produced the sheaf of arrangements he was carrying under one arm and looked at his watch. "Am I early?"

Frankie had a few other things to do, a million places he would rather be, a million ways he would prefer to spend a winter's day than to sit with Boyle and discuss his arrangements. "Oh, your arrangements—" he tried to act surprised. "Look, Boyle, I'm a little busy right now. Some other time."

Boyle gave the two bookkeepers the once-over, his typically fertile mind at once giving rise to vague suspicions that the two elderly gents were not gents at all, but arrangers who had somehow tricked him and gotten to Frankie first. He had exhibited paranoid tendencies for years, but they were becoming more pronounced since he had been in Indiana. Frankie's announcement therefore stunned him.

"Frankie," he said, managing to look both taken aback and belligerent at the same time, "I thought you wanted to look them over. You said if you liked them, you'd let me take the band through a couple of numbers tomorrow—"

"Don't tell me what I said, Boyle. I got other numbers right now—big red ones. Why don't you go out, go practice, go play your saxophone? Just put the arrangements in the chair, move the clothes—I can't get to 'em right now, that's all."

Johnny backed up, the smirk still on his face. He was more convinced than ever that the two men in green sun visors were something other than what they seemed, but he did as Frankie asked. None too happily, he picked up a wad of Frankie's dirty laundry in the chair by the door and put down his arrangements, then stood looking for a place for the clothes, when Paul Wilson unexpectedly stuck his head in the room, quite agitated.

"Frankie, you got a minute?" Paul said, then acknowledged Boyle holding the dirty laundry. "Hi, Boyle. Frankie, you'd better get downstairs. The manager wants to see you. The house dick caught Fowler again in his room with a townie—"

No one knew much about Fowler. He snorted cocaine and stayed out of the way, was rumored to have marital problems. Still, nothing Paul had said so far disturbed Frankie unduly. He saw no reason to become personally involved. Let Fowler handle it. The fellows often coaxed young ladies up to their rooms on the pretext of drinks or cosmopolitan conversation.

"So what?" Frankie said matter-of-factly.

"She's fourteen."

That was a little young, but he'd known younger. Frankie still didn't blink. "So what?" he said.

Paul continued. "Fowler slugged the guy, took away his gun, and he's shooting at the street. You'd better hurry."

So Fowler had flipped out, and by now Frankie quite agreed there was trouble, dropping everything and coming over to get dressed, looking for his clothes in a mad rush.

"The city cops are on the way," Paul said.

That's all he needed. Frankie scrambled, unable to find his trousers. It was always that way—when you needed them, you could never find them. "Where the hell are my pants?" Then he saw Boyle had them. "Gimme those pants, Boyle—no, not those, the other ones—my green ones."

104

Boyle was still holding his clothes. He handed him a pair of pants, and Frankie hopped around, struggling to get into them as he hurried out of the room. . . .

Paul lingered behind just long enough to ask Boyle, "How'd it go with the arrangements?" By now they were of one accord, at least musically. Paul was Boyle's ally, at least musically.

"I couldn't get arrested in this band," Boyle said.

"It's easy. I'll show you how," Paul said, pulling Johnny after him out of the room, leaving only the bookkeepers to stare after them for quite some time until they turned back to their ledgers, finding safety in numbers.

Chapter 6

IN EVERY STORY LIKE THIS, MEANING STORIES ABOUT young newlyweds, the happiness can't go on forever. Otherwise, why tell the story? Life is more than a bed of roses; sticky complications creep into the most idyllic of relationships, and no one ever said Johnny and Francine had one of those. Both had odd talents and uneven tempers, so they already had a built-in complication of a kind involving the kind of work they did, and so forth. But the most common complications, for purposes of drama, are those that come from without and are the most logical—precisely the sort of thing that we as impartial observers might expect, the ever-present threat of the "blessed event" springing immediately to mind. But Boyle didn't think logically. He had fantasies of a future but made no plans for it, and if he ever thought of a "blessed event" coming his way, he banished the thought entirely. It was too logical.

He thought more in terms of the melodramatic. He

had dreams of the bus going over the cliff and the band perishing in flames. Where he was when all this was going on was never clear in the dreams; obviously he was on the nearby cliff and watching, his main agony being that Francine was on the bus and calling out to him, "Johnnnnnnnnnnn—y!" as she went down in a ball of fire. It was always in technicolor, too, which made him wonder at the gruesomeness of it. He would reach out to her and nearly go tumbling over the edge himself but would of course catch himself in time, and feel the accompanying guilt.

Young Genius on the Saxophone Only Survivor in Freak Accident, Wife and Various Unknowns Perish—the papers were full of it. And then he woke up in a sweat.

So, no, he had never given much serious thought to the notion of a "blessed event" falling into his lap and suddenly turning his life around. He hardly thought of himself as human in the first place, so he perhaps considered himself incapable of such a thing. All the same, one day he learned different.

FADE IN . . . members of the band passing the cash register in a Chinese restaurant, picking up mints and chewing them without paying their tabs, simply pointing back at Johnny Boyle who is sitting with Paul Wilson in one of the back booths . . . the musicians indicating to the cashier that Johnny will be paying the bill for all of them.

"The guy back there," one of them says. "The pink shirt, he's getting it." Another adds as he reaches for a toothpick, "The guy with the pink shirt, he's covering it. Delicious."

In the meantime, Paul was talking to Johnny about the future, how it paid to be prepared, Boyle only half listening, preferring to study a piece of sheet music as he sipped his coffee.

"I was a boy scout," Boyle said cryptically.

Paul ignored him. "Something's in the works," he went on. "It don't hurt to make plans—I got a brother in California. Everything's better out there. The service guys liked it so much they're all staying out there—it's geographical good sense. The center of the country is now in Ohio and moving west, something like a hundred yards a week. . . ."

He observed that Boyle was paying even less attention to him than before, Boyle's principal interest at the moment appearing to be Francine's abandoned plate of food sitting next to his elbow, and he began to spear bean sprouts with his fork.

"Where'd she go?" Paul said.

Boyle shrugged. "Went back to the hotel, said her stomach was upset. She's been having indigestion lately."

When Boyle said that, Paul had to blink. It had been said in such an offhand way that a thought crossed his mind. He dismissed the possibility momentarily, but on looking at Boyle, he knew it was true—Boyle didn't know. Now it was Paul's turn to sit there with a smirk on his face, a bemused look of superiority.

"Besides," he told Boyle nonchalantly, "you got your own problems."

"What problems? I ain't got any problems. *What, me worry?*" Boyle was speaking through a mouthful of bean sprouts.

Paul leaned closer as he said in a more confidential tone, "It's OK. Just between you and me, you can talk about it. I already know. She told me."

Boyle stopped chewing. "Told you what?"

"You know."

"No, what? I don't know. What?"

"She must have told you."

"Sure, she told me."

"Well, then you know."

"Know what?"

It was clear they were getting nowhere fast along this route, and just as clear that Boyle was totally in the dark regarding his wife's condition.

"I took her to the doc yesterday," Paul said.

"A doctor? Why? What's going on? She sick?"

"She didn't tell you? She must have told you. You're her husband."

"Of course she told me," Boyle said, standing up with his customary aplomb. "What's the matter, before I bust your mouth—what's she got? What the hell's the matter with her?"

Every eye in the place was turning their way, and Paul tried to get him to sit down, but Boyle had strangely lost his appetite.

"Sit down. Be calm," Paul said.

"Be calm—? She said she's been having stomach trouble. She didn't touch her bean sprouts. She always never did that before. Where'd she go? Is it serious?"

"Sort of serious."

Boyle threw down his napkin, a couple of dimes for a tip, and Paul joined him on his way out. Boyle was walking in a hurry, various clues coming home to rest. Francine had been behaving oddly lately, spending a lot of time in the bathroom, eating a sack of apples daily. Maybe he was sitting through these and other clues and deducing the truth even as he crossed the restaurant, but from the look on his face he was simply concerned and confused.

"How could she do this?" he asked Paul, then, of no one in particular, "How could she do this?"

They had reached the cash register, and Johnny stopped to pay his bill, taking a measly couple of dollars out of his pocket.

"Sure, she told me!" he said, unwilling to admit the truth even up to the last. "She tells me everything." He asked the cashier, "Whadda I owe you?"

These things happen. Paul didn't plan on saying it

precisely this way, or picking this moment. In fact, he shouldn't have even been the one who had to do it, but he said, "She's going to have a baby."

The "blessed event," suddenly. The option Boyle had refused to consider. He turned sharply, looked at Paul with the most helpless of expressions, and just at that moment heard the attendant say, "That'll be forty-eight dollars."

It was the final straw, a combination of factors, but that did it. He blew his top and took a slug at the guy, muttering a form of English. "The fuck you—!"

Luckily, his swing missed, and Paul pulled him away before he could hurt any other innocent persons. Paul paid the bill, and Boyle stomped back to the hotel. That's the way he learned his wife was pregnant.

Chapter 7

THE BUS MOVES ON, BUT EVENTS MOVE FASTER. ONE night when they were crossing the darkened country-side, and everyone else was asleep, Frankie Clarke sat under the glow of his reading lamp. His hair was in turmoil, and he was reading—what else? his customary late-night reading, his collection of green vouchers—when he felt the seat sag beside him and looked to see who it was. Francine had joined him.

"Frankie—you busy? Can I talk to you a minute?" she whispered.

"You good at figures?"

He offered her a cigarette he was lighting and she declined.

"I've been wanting to see you anyway," he said, blowing smoke at the window. "I'm telling everybody else in the morning. I had another week's worth of bookings canceled today."

"You or them?" Her eyes were wide. She could guess what came next and knew it was a senseless question. They had been having dates canceled as little as three days in advance. There wasn't any business. "Which means?" she said.

"Which means, they're canceling me—I'm canceling them first. I'm calling off the tour, as of Friday. We're going home." He offered her another cigarette, not remembering. "You want a cigarette?"

She was thinking, "I don't smoke," she said.

Frankie was thinking, too. It was so quiet, with everyone asleep, and he was beyond depression, feeling philosophical, nostalgic for the good old days. He put away his cigarettes. "That's right," he said. "Nancy was the one that smoked. You're the poet—I get you two mixed up. Written any poems lately?"

She looked at him, put her hand on his arm, having the greatest idea all of a sudden. "Here's one," she said. "Let Johnny take the band/'cause he's the man."

Frankie didn't immediately get the point. Either that or he chose not to. He ignored her plea and nodded, reaching under his seat for a thermos jug. "I hear you're pregnant—I can always tell. Gives you those nice pear-shaped tones. You want some coffee?"

He poured a cup. "I don't drink coffee," she said. It looked lukewarm, anyway.

It all came back to him. "Helen was the one who drank all the coffee," he said. "Don't worry about it, Evans. As many singers as I've had—Mary Wetherill in 1938, married a trombone player—they're alive in Minneapolis. Same thing with Kay Davis, 1942—" He paused to inhale smoke. "So what're your plans?"

"I don't know," she said, not knowing where to begin, so much more to think about suddenly. "That's why I wanted to talk to you, to give you notice—it just

110

seemed the professional thing—I've never been pregnant before."

"Who is it—Boyle?"

"Of course it is."

"Don't you wanna go home?" he said.

"Home? *This* is home. Frankie, look, you said you're gonna cancel the tour anyway, which means you got nothing to lose. *We* could finish the bookings we've still got. You could do whatever you want, go off to Miami, soak your head in Palm Beach, read your stock averages—but the rest of us—why not let us take the band? It's just a few weeks, and you could give a young guy a chance—"

He cut her off. "I know what you're getting at, and there's only one guy who can handle this outfit—"

"Who's that? Johnny?"

"No. Me. Besides, I wouldn't be doing him any favor, believe me. It's nothing but a headache—a headache, and you're pregnant—"

But she protested, "Those pear-shaped tones, Frankie. I won't show for months. My cheeks glow. I look better, the bigger I get. People pay to see fat ladies every day, and listen, Frankie—" And listen, Frankie, now here's what we gotta do. Now listen, Frankie, here's the lowdown. Buzz, buzz. She gave him the spiel. "The guys respect Johnny, they know he's full of new ideas, and they'd be willing to take a pay cut, I know they would—if they had it put to them it's either that or the bread line, which do you think they'd choose?"

Frankie wasn't sure, but it was worth thinking over. He ripped a page from his scratch pad he'd been doodling on and wadded it up, deciding to hand her the problem. He knew which one he'd choose, and he wasn't saying. So he dropped the vouchers in her lap. If Boyle could get some free work out of the lazy bastards, more power to him.

111

"You take these tonight," he said, "look at these figures, and tell me in the morning whether you're still willing to work for nothing to pay my bills. I'm going to bed."

He reached up and flipped off the reading lamp, curling up in his blanket like a fetus. She didn't move.

"Frankie, I can tell you now," she said.

He turned to look at her. He'd never met anyone quite like her before, and to think that in the beginning he'd thought her homely and odd-looking. Funny how in the darkness she had it over all the others. Her large dark eyes shone brightly, and she exuded a sensuality that awoke in him certain incestuous feelings.

"You're quite a girl," he said. "What would you like me to do?"

"Sprinkle your water, Frankie."

"Sprinkle my water?"

"Give Johnny your blessing."

He sat up for a minute and managed a smile. Then before he knew what he was doing, he kissed her. They both backed off and looked at each other. There hadn't been anything to it, but even so he felt foolish, alibiing his way clear in a fatherly tone, "You know, those other singers of mine—I'd say you were the best. Anything else or can I turn in now?"

To his delight, she returned his kiss on the forehead and tucked him in for the night, saying, "You keep getting cuter, Frankie. There oughtta be a law against older men."

Well, it was mixed emotions. The older man shut his eyes, and the affair was over. She went back to her husband, and he conked out in the seat.

Chapter 8

IN SOUTH BEND, INDIANA, THE JUKEBOX WAS PLAYING "Billets-Doux" by Django Reinhardt. It was the twilight world of a college all-night diner, a purple-and-gold Notre Dame banner on the wall and snowflakes drifting by the window. Bing Crosby was sitting at the counter with Frank Leahy, and Johnny and Francine shared a booth, conversing softly. She was looking at his palm, squeezing his fingers together, those lovely long fingers. He had nicer hands than hers.

"No kidding, Johnny," she said, "he looked just like Lionel Barrymore. His hands were very warm, and he took mine in his and started to explain just like old Gillespie—"

"Dizzy Gillespie—?" Boyle said, freely associating.

"*Doctor* Gillespie—explaining the miracle of life, the pollinated germ, the incredible saga of it all—"

Boyle was thinking of just that, the saga, as he sipped his coffee.

"The saga of it is, you didn't even tell me first," he said. "I learn about it a month later from one of your old boyfriends."

"We've been over that."

"Felix, the bus driver, said he knew before I did."

She didn't dispute it. "I'm sure I told you, probably late one night when we were in bed. You probably just forgot."

"I could have been asleep, I guess," he admitted, though he really admitted no such thing. They'd had this same conversation dozens of times. Each time she attempted to steer it one way, he'd steer it another. Whenever she wanted to get serious and talk turkey,

113

Boyle lapsed into self-pity, that sort of mumbling arrangement he had with the world when things didn't go to suit him.

"Yeah, that's when it was," she said. "One night when you were sleeping. Johnny, what I'm saying—what he told me—is it's so normal, just like pouring your coffee, it's that normal."

"Do I look normal to you?" he said.

"You never looked normal to me."

Francine was suddenly June Allyson with that glistening look in her eyes. All my life I've wanted to be normal, she thought. All I really want is a garden and a man. Tap dancing at the age of five . . . "Just keep dancing" . . . voice lessons, a trip to New York for Major Bowes, high school drama—but only the sort that takes place on stage. She missed getting firsthand experience in secondhand cars, the whole teen-age thing. She sang weekends, didn't have a real date till the senior prom.

"You don't look normal to me, neither," Boyle said. "A baby, it just never occurred to me—a kid—I don't know where to put it—a little thing like that turns our whole lives on its head—and you didn't even tell me first."

"We've been over that, Johnny. I want it, Johnny—I'm Catholic, and I make good money."

He waved his hamburger, begging to differ on a small point.

"I wouldn't have it any other way," he said. "But you're not making that kind of dough any more. You're taking a fifty percent cut—"

"Fifty percent?" She shuddered. "I know the band's in trouble, but—why all of it outta me? Why not cut some of the fat lard-bottoms in the back row? I work hard for my money!" It was a masterful performance. She was very convincing in her ignorance of the currents she herself had set in motion with her late-night

114

chat with Frankie on the bus. She sure fooled Boyle. "I'll talk to Frankie!" she said.

Then he said, "Frankie ain't calling the shots. I am."

It couldn't have been more than a minute that they stared at one another without a word being spoken, but it was their finest hour anyway, and it belonged to her. She had the satisfaction of knowing, whether he ever would or not. That's just the way she was. She never would have broken the news to him first, but instead feigned surprise. He confirmed it. "Yeah, Frankie's throwing in the towel," he said. "The guys are handing me the band if I want it—no joke."

She was elated, though there were a couple of facts needing straightening out. It was doubtful that the guys in the band would have elected Boyle dogcatcher if Frankie hadn't gone behind the scenes and laid it on the line to them. It was Boyle or nothing at all, and even at that, it was a close race. For all her other qualities, Francine had a blind spot; she never quite understood other people's opinion of Boyle, and those who loved her wouldn't tell her for fear of getting on her bad side. If she was in your corner, she was in your corner—that's all there was to it, and to hell with objectivity. She was a friend, and a passionate booster.

"If you want it!" she exclaimed. "The only thing in your life you were ever meant for, the only thing you ever wanted—a band, musicians, your own music—a band and a bus—where's the phone? Who do I call? Whadda you mean—*if?*"

Boyle, who could always find a dark cloud in every silver lining: "Yeah, but the baby—looking up the road a ways, the kid's gotta be near its mother. The way things work out, you never know—"

"No guaranteed gates, if that's what you mean," she said, on the verge of pounding the table for emphasis. "No guaranteed gates in life—but, Johnny, you're just scared. That's it."

And there was some truth in that. Glad tidings and blessed events scared the piss out of Boyle. Today the psychologists would have a word for it. Boyle didn't have a successful "mental picture" of himself. How could you be successful and persecuted at the same time? One had to make a choice.

"Maybe Boston would be best," he said cautiously.

"Boston? Who do I know in Boston? My mother's dead."

"Yeah, but—just go back and wait—I'll look around for something. Maybe not music, but something'll pop up—I'll work in a factory with my hands—"

What the hell was he talking about? With his lily-white hands? Obviously he was relatively sincere, just a mile off base, feeling all kinds of sorry for the both of them, looking down at the table . . . as she reached over and raised his chin. His eyes were getting moist for the third time in his life. Then, starting out softly, she laid down the law.

"You would leave this?" she said, flicking away her own tears. "Go back to 'wherever' with me, forgetting this, everything you want, forgetting what we've talked about—I mean that much to you?" He didn't say yes, but she didn't give him a chance. Finally, she hit the table, slapping it suddenly. "Well, I got news for you, kid," she told him. "You can't go back, whether you like it or not—I won't let you do it—and that's mother's milk talking."

Boyle was overcome. As he bit into his hamburger, he was weeping uncontrollably.

"I love you, I swear," he said. "I love you—God."

"I love you, too. Whadda you want?"

He was looking around for something. "The catsup," he said.

She handed him the catsup and watched as he opened it and proceeded to pound on the bottom of the

116

bottle, waiting impatiently for the stuff to come out. He was still crying, his tears falling in the fried potatoes. It was the most touching thing she had ever seen.

"First time I ever met you," he said, "I knew. I knew. I came to this band—I knew. People think I act nuts, but I knew—if you *know*, if you really *know*, you can do whatever you want, and the hell with them. I wrote you the letters, every day after you skipped New York—"

For the first time, something didn't ring quite true. Here she was, enjoying the tenderness of the moment, but facts were facts, and Boyle had his a little confused.

"I didn't skip New York," she said, and she didn't recall any letters.

"Why didn't you answer my letters?"

"What letters? You didn't write to me," she said. She wasn't going to let him get away with this one. "You never wrote—don't tell me you wrote."

And to her relief he didn't argue. "See, you know, too," he said and smiled, wiping his eyes. "That's why I love you, 'cause you know."

While she was trying to figure out what he meant by that, he signaled the waitress. He was still getting nowhere with the catsup and didn't intend to wait all night. He had things to do, people to see.

"Waitress, put some catsup on this, will you?"

Francine was still mulling over the other, trying to figure out what he had meant when he said, "That's why I love you, 'cause you know." All she could think of was that she didn't let his bullshit pass without putting him in his place. She didn't take a lot of guff from him, and maybe that was what he meant, but just then the catsup finally spurted out of the bottle and ran all over his white shirt. A more timid individual would have been beset by anxiety, but Boyle handled himself calmly and without raising a stink, as befitted a natural leader.

"Never mind," he told the waitress. "I fixed it."

Chapter 9

THE NEXT STOP WAS CHICAGO AND THE HOTEL Sherman on a lunch hour. People, extras, were passing on the sidewalk in a preview of '46 spring fashions, and a hotel employee brought out the latest placard to insert in the glass case, under the heading, *Now Appearing*. It was one of those same awful posters seen at The Greenbrier and every other stop along the way, the one with Frankie Clark's ten-year-old eight-by-ten and the prewar smile.

Frankie Clark and His Orchestra, Exclusive Two Week Engagement. Well, if they had him, it was exclusive all right, because Frankie wasn't playing there or anywhere else. He was somewhere in Florida's citrus league, watching the Dodgers loosen up. Obviously, word of this had been slow to reach the appropriate high places, but the man with the sign had a mind of his own and elected to follow his intuition. He had had considerable experience in this area, was acquainted with most of the major dance bands personally, and just to be on the safe side, instead of putting up the placard, he headed inside to get the poop.

He crossed the busy lobby, still wielding the unwieldy sign and bumping into ashtrays, but when he reached the ballroom, he knew his original hunch had been correct. It was just as he had thought, and he wasn't alone in his misgivings. Mr. Horace Morris of the hotel staff was also there, as was the Johnny Boyle Orchestra.

It all looked disorganized, and it was. The band was on the bandstand, perspiring in shirt-sleeves and looking out across a gilded hallowed hall that in the annals of dance banddom had seen them all over the years, had seen the great ones come and go, but never anything like the outfit fronted by Johnny Boyle, vaunted master of mayhem. I mean, what else could you call it? For starters, he had sent the band through a cram course of his arrangements, insane pieces of music marked by the heavy use of the word "improvisation." To understand how poorly the guys played it, you have to use another word, "imagination." Boyle couldn't understand it. He didn't know that some of his charges had been playing since Paul Whiteman's days without improvising anything more than a martini, and he was somewhat frustrated on this blustery Chicago afternoon. He was actually feeling down at the mouth but was compelled by circumstances to be blustery himself, in defense of his own efforts. Sitting at a table nearby was Mr. Horace Morris, Midwestern sophisticate and boulevardier, also empowered to book entertainment for the hotel. It was on his say-so that the fate of the Johnny Boyle Band now rode, crested, or fell, and when Boyle wasn't yelling at his men, he was giving Mr. Morris a dose of his brand of charm.

"I know it's different," he said. "It ain't the old Frankie Clarke, for one thing—but so what? It's gonna get modern. We got a lot of potential in this outfit but a lot of insecurity at the same time, a lot of guys groping in the dark for something and they ain't sure what. We got all new charts, new ideas, but a week from now you won't even remember Frankie Clarke—"

Mr. Morris was game. "I don't remember him now," he said. "But who are you?" To himself, he thought, This s.o.b.'s crazy.

"You like bop?"

"What is bop?"

Boyle could have told him what bop was, starting with Monk's emphasis on the right hand while the bass took the left, or it was Charlie Christian's electric guitar—the *late* Charlie Christian on the first electric guitar and the late Jimmy Blanton on bass, two young lions killed in their twenties by TB—or it was Lester "Prez" Young, President of the Saxophones, and certainly it was Charlie Parker, king of the boppers. The Bird was the Word.

But Boyle saved his breath. He could tell by looking that it was a waste of time, noting that Mr. Morris was having extreme difficulty in stifling a yawn at all this talk of musical theory and the wave of the future.

"The future is now," someone has said, and "Give me entertainment," said the impresario, his hand covering his mouth. "That's what the people want."

And Boyle felt the same himself. They only differed as to what constituted entertainment. Still, a demonstration was always better than a thousand words, and he took a step onto the shiny dance floor to call up to the bandstand, "Paul, let's hear 'Nice Work if You Can Get It' for Mr. Horace." The title was an ironic one on this of all days, but it was also one of their best charts, a Gershwin tune everyone knew even in boppish dress. There was one difficulty—Mr. Morris wasn't "Mr. Horace" and he resented it when he was.

"I told you," he said. "It's Morris."

Paul, too, chimed in with the correction, telling Boyle, "It's Morris, Johnny."

Boyle nodded, a big enough fellow to admit a mistake. "All right, let's hear it for Morris," he said.

"Mr. Morris. Horace Morris," said Mr. Horace Morris, getting to his feet finally. He had just about had enough. "Horace is my first name. I don't like the whole idea—never mind the song—this new music, where'd it come from? I thought I was hiring Frankie Clarke, and I thought he had a singer."

It was remarkable to see the way Boyle could turn on a dime when the situation demanded it, like those Oriental fighters—practitioners of the art of nonresistance. Take the opponent's motion and go with it, thus throwing him off balance, which was exactly what Boyle did. "Now that's savvy, Mr. Morris," he said as though he couldn't agree more. "Like I say, forget the band. Forget the band, Horace, forget the music, forget the notes—it's the singers the public wants. That's it nowadays—nice hairdos, a voice with curves, dolls—you got me? I got a singer for you. Francine Evans! Francine—"

He called loudly, hoping she would hear him backstage. She had been disappearing mysteriously lately, but at least in this case it was planned. He had expected her to be his secret weapon when all else failed, and it looked like all else would. Once again, like back at the Palm Club in Brooklyn, it was up to her to pull his chestnuts out of the fire, and in the meantime Mr. Morris had the temerity to ask, "Is she stunning?"

"Stunning, for you." Boyle's eyes scanned the bandstand. Where was she? What was keeping her? "Tall, blonde, long blond hair—sometimes. You'll love her. And she steps out. There she is now."

Francine had stepped out, it was true, but she looked less than stunning. She was tired and looked it. Frankly, she was worn out. She hadn't had much sleep the night before, had spent it mostly in the bathroom, and now, as she took her professional pose wearily on the stool with the microphone, she asked him, "What'll it be?"

Her face was drooping, and even Boyle was a little astonished at her appearance. " 'The Man I Love,' " he said. It was the first thing that came to mind.

And what if she didn't look so hot? She was still a helluva secret weapon. When she opened her mouth to sing, you forgot all about the rest of her, but you didn't forget that voice. You went out to tell your friends about it. "Remember the name," you said, and that's what Horace Morris said to the hotel employee who had come into the ballroom with the Frankie Clarke placard.

"Put that away," Mr. Morris told him as they stood near the back and listened, and the hotel employee put away his sign, that old-fashioned relic of the big-band heyday when band leaders amounted to something. Now it was singers, just like Boyle had said. America wanted its sweethearts, and after Horace Morris had heard her third song, he knew he would be hearing a lot more. We all would. "Francine Evans," he said, to hear the sound of it. "Remember the name."

And of course the man did. For evidence of that, CUT TO a few nights later, EXTERIOR HOTEL SHERMAN—NIGHT, Francine's VOICE OVER her photograph—the photograph that had replaced Frankie Clarke's as the star of the show, not to mention first billing. It was just a sign of the times. *Francine Evans,* the sign read, *Appearing with the Johnny Doyle Orchestra.* And that was how Johnny Boyle became Johnny Doyle. He didn't mind, he sort of liked the switch. He was tired of his old name, and maybe he needed a new one for the new plateau on which he now found himself. The old Johnny Boyle was a thing of the past, although of course he wasn't. Still, people persist in making statements such as that, dividing their lives into chapters, pretending to make clean breaks with the past, when this so seldom happens. Johnny Boyle would always be Johnny Boyle, and he didn't need a name anyway. People always called him "Asshole," which was a way of saying that he was known, though he did sort of miss star billing. I say "missed"—but how can you miss what you've never had? All the same, Boyle missed it, and a lesser man might have resented her.

122

MORE MONTAGE, shots of couples getting out of taxis to go inside the hotel, but for all of that, traffic was light. Francine was still a local newcomer and word had yet to get around, the same song continuing inside the ballroom where Francine was at the mike and clearly in her natural element, like a fish in water.

She was ever the trouper, trying tonight as always to establish some rapport with the audience sitting out in the dark. "Hi, I'm Francine Evans from the Red Cross," she said. "Anybody here give?" Silence. "Anybody here bleed?" Silence. "Anybody here from Chicago?"

Came a throaty voice from the back: "This *is* Chicago. Hell!"

She licked her lips but kept the old poise. "You said it. Just keeping you on your toes," she said, repeating to herself the immortal words of her tap teacher. "Just keep dancing. Just keep dancing."

But while reciting under her breath, she was interrupted by a rude individual tugging on the hem of her skirt. For a moment she almost thought she was in danger of losing it, as she looked down to see a strikingly handsome fellow without a mark on his olive face, tough-looking and very smooth in a dinner jacket. He was obviously a Chicago hoodlum on his way up the underworld ladder. He pressed a ten-dollar bill in her hand.

"Hey, doll, do my sweetie a favor," he said. "Play 'Don't Get Around Much Anymore'—it used to be her old man's favorite before he passed on."

"I don't know that we do that one," she replied, but with a smile.

"You learn it. You play it, I'll get you some business. You're nice. I like you."

Well, he wasn't so bad himself—and Francine shook hands with him. "It's starting to get familiar," she said, turning back to bandleader Johnny. "Johnny—"

All that night Johnny couldn't sleep. He spent most of the night at the window, looking like Humphrey Bogart in the shadows, smoking a cigarette and staring at the twinkling lights of the city through gauze curtains. A dark figure in silhouette, a wanted man holed up, a private eye staking out the building across the street. There was bustling Chicago spread below him, gangster capital of the world, and Boyle had seen enough movies to know what happened now. He had seen the hoodlum approach the bandstand and press the money into Francine's palm. The whole band had been whispering as the rumor made the rounds that somebody "big" was in the audience. Boyle himself had seen the way the torpedo looked at Francine, and soon he would be getting a call.

The phone on the nightstand would ring, and he would say, "Yes, this is Johnny Boyle, I mean Doyle, Jimmy Doyle. Who is this?"

Thus having concealed his real name from the other party, he would listen carefully, beads of sweat popping out on his forehead. The voice at the other end grated like gravel. "I'm calling for a friend of a friend, Johnny baby. Mr. Antonelli would like to see you, Johnny. He was at the show tonight, and he liked your music. He liked it so much he'd like to get in on a piece of the action."

Boyle gulped and continued staring out the window, hearing the mob's quaint little euphemisms in his head. "A piece of the action." Chicago, USA. He knew they were out there somewhere, and of course they were. He had no doubts they would play rough if he didn't go along, might do him like they had done Joe E. Brown twenty years before and rip his throat from ear to ear. How would that be, his wife expecting their first child . . . ? He shuddered to think of it.

And of course he might have had a point. He might have been right, and they might have done that, if these had been the old days. But they weren't, and the mob long ago had had enough sense to realize that big bands were on their way out and, quite frankly, weren't worth the bother.

Several hours later the sun was creeping up and the phone still hadn't rung. The mob had yet to be heard from, and Boyle finally decided to get back into bed, telling himself none too convincingly he was merely imagining things.

"Johnny, what's the matter?" Francine asked him sleepily.

And instead of himself he began to think of her. Of course, that was the way the mob worked. They wouldn't waste time with him—they would go for her. The mob always went for your wife and kid, not to mention the kind of brilliant future his wife had in this business. I mean, realistically, her future was more promising than his own. He would never even be here if it weren't for her, he thought, as he looked over and admired her sleeping form, her arm outside the covers. He touched her and instantly thought of Peggy Lee in the role, the great Peggy Lee intimidated and destroyed by certain gangsters who owned her. Imagine his surprise years later when he walked into a theater in N.Y. and saw *Pete Kelly's Blues,* a movie in which substantially the same thing happened.

The next day in rehearsals, Boyle was even more volatile than his usual self, from the lack of sleep the night before. Francine was singing "Taking a Chance On Love," and he was typically involved in a dozen things at once, and to Boyle, being involved meant running the show, whipping through an arrangement at the same time he ate a sandwich, and now waving the band to a screeching halt, much to Francine's displeasure.

"What now?" she beseeched him. "Johnny, it's one song for two hours—"

"Do you like the way it sounds?" he demanded.

"It sounds OK, as good as we're gonna get it."

"It don't sound OK when I'm hearing what I'm hearing. What am I standing out here for, waving my hands like an idiot? Am I entertaining you guys, or the other way around? That ain't quite it! I said it before, and I'll say it—"

He would have said it again, except that the drummer, Nicky Redovich, was flicking the snares on his snare drum so loudly that it interrupted the great man's train of thought.

"Will you shut up?" Johnny yelled at him, blowing his cool. "You're part of the problem, Nicky. The licks you're playing—"

Nicky, in no better mood, shot back, "They're good licks! I know how to play—they're outstanding licks!"

"Yeah? I don't want your licks!" Boyle shouted. "There's a guy in town tonight. I want you to do me a favor—"

"Ha!"

"I want you to do me a favor and go hear him *after* we're done—his name's Max Roach. He plays the kind of drums we're after—"

Nicky didn't have to sit there and take that kind of abuse like a shmuck, so he did what any red-blooded drummer would do. He threw his drumsticks at Johnny Boyle and threatened to tear up his arrangement.

"I got a better idea!" he said. "Why don't you hire him? Why don't you go with a whole new band, 'cause I am! I quit!"

"Yeah, that's it! Quit!" Boyle was jumping up and down, his face mauve, the color of the carpet he was stomping the dust out of. "Don't learn nothing! Stay in your set ways, you creep! Be gutless!" he taunted. "We're trying to make music here, something new to

126

you. You don't wanna see Max Roach 'cause he's the best, and the best scares you!"

"Johnny—" It was Francine, cutting in, and someone had to before they came to blows. "Johnny—Nicky—just wait a minute!"

"Francine, this ain't yours," Boyle said.

"Whadda you mean, it's not mine?" she said, getting a little mauve herself. "It's not all yours, you know. The rest of us still work here, too, you know. C'mere a minute."

It was a reasonable enough request, not spoken in a threatening way, but this was one of those times when human beings struck Boyle as pitifully ludicrous and worthless, and he refused to compromise. He told himself it was for the sake of art that he refused to take so much as a half step in her direction.

Instead, he suggested, "Why don't you come here?"

This was more than she had bargained for. She hadn't realized he would make such a big deal out of it. They were husband and wife, after all. They should be able to handle these trivial matters, but she wasn't about to be the first one to knuckle under in front of these witnesses, now that he had made it a struggle of personalities.

"I'm at the microphone," she said into the microphone in a low, growling voice. "C'mere, Johnny."

"No. You come over here."

It was absurd, but there it was, a Mexican standoff at the OK Corral, and whatever the original subject of dispute had been, it was by now forgotten, the guys in the band setting everything else aside to watch the titans clash . . . Johnny and Francine, bulls locking horns, rhino vs hippo, one of nature's classic duels for primacy, and neither was about to yield an inch. Francine felt their eyes on her and felt her spine stiffen resolutely, and no wonder—the hopes of reasonable-thinking people everywhere were on her shoulders, the hopes of Nicky Redovich in particular, the latter providing her with a soul-stirring drum roll in the best USO fighting tradition.

"Johnny, come here," she said.

"*You* come here. Who's the leader?"

What insolence! She couldn't believe it. " 'Who's on first? What's on second?' " she said, recalling a similar circular argument of Abbott and Costello's that seemed never to end. "My feet are tired. Come here, Johnny, please."

It was the first time she had used the word "please," and the last time, as far as she was concerned, for all the good it did.

"Make me," he said, like a pouting kid in the playground. "Make me."

Well, if that was the way he wanted it, she had a ready response. Fuming, she simply pushed over the microphone stand and walked away, the mike hitting the floor behind her with a thunderous roar over the p.a. as she headed across the dance floor, not even caring to look back when he called after her. He still hadn't budged from his spot, which she supposed made him the unofficial winner of sorts, but they would see about that.

"Trying to push your weight around?" he yelled after her. "Pretty soon you'll be big enough—"

He referred to her physical person, and it could have gotten uglier from there. She was on the verge of whirling and letting him really have it—and she was the one person who could—when just at that moment she ran into Paul Wilson, good old Paul, who had just entered the ballroom from the lobby and was advancing across the dance floor at full throttle, a couple of newspapers under each arm. She couldn't remember when she had seen him so excited.

"Francine, where're you going?" he exclaimed, reaching out to give her a squeeze, all bubbly. "You

seen the reviews? You made the papers—all of 'em—
all raves. They love you! Johnny—"

Johnny indeed seemed the next logical person to tell.
He was watching from the bandstand as Paul waved
the papers like mad. In his mind's eye, Paul didn't
seem near at all, but suddenly far away, his voice coming from a distance over a long period of time, the
dance floor wide as the Big Muddy, the two of them on
opposite shores. All at once Boyle realized he didn't
know this person, or what either of them was doing
there.

"Johnny, you see the papers?" Paul shouted, his enthusiasm undiminished. "C'mere."

"No. You come here."

In other words, Boyle still wasn't moving. Unlike
Mohammed, the mountain would have to come to him.
Paul didn't know what to make of his oddball behavior, but that was nothing new, and, besides, Boyle
wasn't worth spoiling an afternoon over, especially this
one. There was too much to celebrate. "We're a
smash!" he said. "Chicago eats us up! It's in the papers—"

Triggered by the good news, the band went bananas,
everybody leaving their seats to hurry over to where
Paul was and get a look at the reviews—everybody,
that is, except Johnny, who subsequently trailed behind. But at least he moved off his damned spot.

An hour later everyone had gone for drinks except
Johnny and Francine, the two of them sitting together
on the piano bench in a melancholy mood. What was
past was forgotten, but always just below the surface.
Her head reclined on his shoulder, and he stuck a cigarette in his mouth, slightly resembling Artie Shaw with
his tie loosened. A copy of one of the Chicago papers
rested atop the piano, the rave review offering up a
picture of Francine at the microphone, her name head-

ing the piece. It was quite flattering. Paul hadn't exaggerated.

Johnny was plunking a few notes of his latest, as Francine played a different melody at the other end of the keyboard. After a while she stopped and watched him erase the old notes and scribble new ones.

"Can Tyson play that?" she said.

"What'd you say?" he said, all wrapped up in what he was doing, the metaphysical difference between an augmented sixth and a seventh major.

"I said it's nice, but do you think Tyson can play it?" she said.

"I don't know. Maybe I'll take off his octave key—Whadda you think?"

"I think it's a swell idea. It sounds terrific," she replied, knowing the way to his heart. "I think it sounds even better than the version you had before—that he couldn't play either."

"Yeah?"

"Yeah, if he can play it."

When she said that, he got discouraged again, dropping his pencil in frustration. He had this thing, a fetish almost, about the lower register of the saxophone. If there had been a religion with a saxophone as godhead, Boyle would have prayed in the lower register. Tyson, on the other hand, played sax, but not all of it. He couldn't get down in the lower depths, and he blamed this inability on various factors, an elusive war wound topping his list of possibles. It drove Boyle up a wall to see his chosen instrument played at less than its potential, and he held that he had at last hit upon the solution. He would remove Tyson's octave key, and no one would be the wiser, probably not even Tyson.

"Anyway, what's the difference?" he said, gloom hanging from his dark eyelashes. "Nobody listens anyway—it's just the band—the whole review, and not a word about any of the new things we're doing. We're just a bunch of jerks—no pretty face, no big production—"

"Sorry I got all the ink," she said, and meant it.

He nodded in sympathy for himself and got up and took his coat, giving her a kiss on the top of her head. "Nah, it's great. I'm proud of you," he said. Then something in her appearance gave him pause. Probably it was the moisture on her cheek when his hand brushed it, the unexpected drop in temperature since last he visited. "You don't look so good. How do you feel?" he said.

"I don't feel so good," she said, inclined to agree.

"How about a matinee?"

It was the best idea she'd heard all day. "I'd love it," she said.

But he had a different kind of matinee in mind than the kind to which they had become accustomed. "No, I mean the movies," he said, his smile deserting him in favor of something more solemn. "I just wanna be by myself awhile. I wanna walk around."

On that curious note he walked away. She looked after him, hurt, uncertain, but certain of one thing as her stomach grumbled a thought. He had known very well what kind of "matinee" she would think he meant. He had said it to be cruel.

Chapter 10

THE CARD OUTSIDE THE HOTEL READ FRANCINE EVANS, *Third Big Week* . . . and inside the band was going to town in full-dress boogie. Attendance had lately come around, and couples were often seen dancing. When a song ended, they actually applauded as Johnny Doyle, a.k.a. Boyle, stepped to the microphone with the world-famous band leader's smile on his face. If you've watched Lawrence Welk on the tube, you've all seen it. Johnny had lately learned that this was the most difficult part of his duties, this practiced smile in the easy manner of one who is at home. It had taken him longer to master the band leader's smile than anything else, but now he was here, at the peak of his form. These days he could outsmile any of them. He'd like to see Frankie Clark try to outsmile him now. Bring on Harry James, Benny Goodman, even the great colored smilers like Basie. He was ready for them on a night like tonight.

"Thank you," he said into the microphone as the applause died. "Thank you very much. We'd like to introduce you now to a hopping new arrangement of an old composition, 'Let's Fall in Love'—and here to do the honors, Miss Francine Evans—I see her coming this way now—a young singer from New England who's really going places—Francine—"

She arrived a moment late, causing Johnny to frown at her as the house lights dimmed and she moved to the mike, steady as she went, doing a voice intro to lead the band in.

"Key of F, gentlemen. Two-quarter time. Ba dop bop, bop doo wop—"

After a couple of bars the gang joined in—so far, so good. In fact, to impartial observers, it was the best they ever sounded together. She threw every ounce of herself into Boyle's fearless bebop arrangement, improvising in and out, her voice as "another instrument" keeping her in the ballpark, carrying on a running banter between herself and the guys.

But about halfway through the tune, the look on her face changed, and it became clear something was up. Suddenly, she wasn't up to par. She must have felt it herself, for she turned urgently to Johnny, trying to get his attention without success. Failing that, she ended the verse abruptly with an awkward gesture, pointing back to Nicky on drums and catching her breath, as she was desperately short of it.

"Ladies and gentlemen," she announced over the mike, introducing Nicky without warning, much to his surprise, "Nicky Redovich on drums—a big hand— Hit it, Nicky!"

Nicky simply looked out of it, a typical drummer's expression, having no idea what was going on, except that the band was now cruising lamely through a vocal without a singer. Looking to Johnny, he hit the drums with a shrug and launched into a furious solo, as impromptu as Johnny's stepping to the mike and watching Francine desert the bandstand and head across the floor to the nearest sanctuary, walking irregularly toward the kitchen.

"Well," Johnny, the spotlight on him, said with a nervous grin, and who could blame him, "I said she was going places, and she certainly has."

The line got a laugh or two, but Boyle didn't titter. Instead, he did the sensible thing and looked worried. He knew he had to do something quick but didn't know what. He glanced around, then left Paul with the band and went after her, pushing his way through the swinging kitchen doors, knowing in his heart that he had no idea what to do when he got there but knowing he had to make a fool of himself all the same. Part of this included sounding angry, for lack of knowing what else to do. "What's the idea? Francine?"

Then he stopped in his tracks, seeing a cluster of black women gathered round—kitchen workers who had cordoned her off and were now handing hot towels back and forth. One of them, holding a mop with the dignity of a queen, spotted him just as he was about to get hysterical.

"Francine—" What could he do but call her name? He had nothing to offer, no suggestions whatever. He

133

was merely going by the husband's handbook, pushing his weight around, until the woman pushed him back.

"She's all right," she said, shaking the mop at him. "You go on now. Get out."

"I'm her husband." He tried to peer around her, but the queen was heavy, and he didn't get far.

"That don't matter. You go on now, just leave her be," she said, and she came within an inch of prodding him with the mop. "Get a doctor."

He didn't need any more prodding. He heard Francine groan on the cold linoleum, and he backed up in a hurry and went to do as he was told.

Later, he was sitting by her bed in a strange room. A blanket was pulled up to her chin. The doctor had come and gone. Her eyes, those bright windows, were open and staring at the ceiling and beyond at nothing in particular. She felt his hand in hers, and that was enough.

"And then I said—it wasn't too clever—" She smiled, thinking back, wondering if this was the time when your life flashed before your eyes—or worse, what if it had already flashed and in her grogginess she had simply missed it? Anyway, she didn't know it then, but she could always read the book years later. " 'Fleas, monsieur,' " she said in a rush of fond memories. " 'Fleas, monsieur? You mean flies.' Or 'Someone opened the window, and influenza'— Get it? In flew Enza? 'How's your wife—compared to what?' Or the three little morons who went to the moon, and—" Here she paused and looked at him to be sure he was listening, even though she was speaking the most perfect nonsense. His face was wrinkled up like a dried washcloth, hanging on her every word, and it was that little boy in him that she had to tell. "Oh, Johnny, my casual love—"

He moved closer, putting himself next to her all

over, snuggling his head on her chest as she bit his hand, squeezed him harder. Her teeth hurt him, but he didn't cry out. He would bite her back when she felt better.

"Johnny, if I never tell you again, I love you forever," she said. "I'm just afraid—"

"Whadda you mean—if you never tell me again? I'll tell you every day. I love you, Francine."

"Weren't you ever in a play?" she said, sponging her tears with his hand. "A high school play?"

"Yeah, sure I was. Who wasn't?"

Her eyes were glistening. "What part? What part did you have?"

"Myself," he said. "A special role. *Volpone* by Ben Jonson, it was our class play, and they couldn't figure out where to put me, so they gave me a special part. 'Johnny Boyle, Appearing as Himself.' "

"As himself." She could see it now. "I can imagine." Her voice trailed off into the past, as she remembered what seemed so long ago and really wasn't. "A boy I went out with—we were the top two in drama class— the boy that played the crazy butler—always so crazy, just a barrel of laughs. I never saw him when we weren't laughing—" A beat, her face collapsing like a broken main, more waterworks down her cheeks, and now Boyle had started, too. He had serious moral reservations about crying. He had dropped bombs on cities and laughed all the way home, so he felt it wasn't the proper thing for a man to do. But he was doing it, telling himself it was just because it made her feel better. Two's company, etcetera.

"Where's he now?" he said.

"Where's who?"

"The crazy butler."

"Oh, he's dead," she said, almost as an afterthought, as though she had thought it would be perfectly obvious. There were so many of them from her own high

135

school. "He's killed now—" as though it were temporary—"somewhere in the Euripides, the New Hebrides—I don't know—God."

Maybe God knew, and maybe He didn't. At the moment there was only Johnny, and he pulled her closer, knowing how she felt. He had lost buddies, a real gone generation. He looked around for something to wipe his nose with and wasn't particular.

"I'm sorry," she said. "I wasn't going to let it get like this. Just tell you like I'm pouring your coffee, plain and simple. I'm going back to New York. You'll have to have the baby without me—I mean—"

He nodded, knowing what she was trying to say. Only one thing bothered him. "Why didn't you tell me before?" He was hurt she hadn't told him, just like she had kept from him the news of her pregnancy itself. "Why didn't you tell me you were having special problems?"

" 'Cause I didn't wanna go—I knew you wouldn't let me stay with the band—"

"Sure, I'd let you. I'd make you. We need you." He was smiling, thank goodness.

"You'll be all right without me."

"Sure, Johnny Boyle and the Swinging Zacatecas." It was a name that had just occurred to him. "Who wants to hear that? Nowadays, without a singer . . ." He was starting to depress her, and he didn't want that. "We'll be all right," he said.

"C'mon, Johnny, where's the old confidence? Say it like you mean it. You promised me. I want a job when I get up, preferably my old one—" She looked at him, cupping his chin in her hands, that wonderful mouth of his that almost had tiny eyes like a separate person. "Geez, I'm sick of looking at you," she said with a sigh of mock disgust. "I don't wanna see you for weeks. Goodnight."

She closed her eyes, rolling her eyeballs up, as he

gave her a kiss and then stepped back from the bed, watching her uneasily, something white in his hand on which he had blown his nose. She wouldn't have seen him, except in the dark her eyes were cheating.

"Johnny, could I have my panties?" she said.

To his bewilderment, he discovered that he was slipping a pair of wartime cotton panties into his jacket, and he wondered why. Then recalling that he had blown his nose on them, he extracted them suddenly, pulling them full-blown from his breast pocket like a Houdini.

"Where's my handkerchief?" he said.

"I don't know, Johnny. You're a big boy now. You've gotta learn to keep up with your things because someday I won't be around."

All of that was true, but it didn't make it any easier. In fact, it had just the opposite effect. On the verge of a tearful relapse, she shut her eyes and sniffed as he gently returned her panties to the bed and removed to the door. She heard his footsteps retreating, and looking at him just once more she said, "We've gotta work on our goodbyes."

He seemed to nod as he went out the door.

NEW YORK, NEW YORK

Chapter 1

WAITING FAITHFULLY BACK AT THE TRAIN STATION IN New York, it was as if Tony Harwell hadn't gone home for these several months. He looked exactly the same, pacing up and down the platform, steam still hissing from the train's undercarriage as people began to disembark. He looked for her everywhere, craning his neck, but didn't see her, then heard a faint voice from behind.

"Tony."

He turned and in the crowd still didn't see her, didn't see her with the porter who was at that moment assisting her from the train. Though freshly made up, she looked simply awful, like a survival case from war-torn Europe. She had lost weight because she hadn't eaten, or what she had eaten she hadn't been able to keep down, her clothes didn't fit, and the trip had sapped her color. Even if Tony had spotted her at first, he would have had to look twice to be sure. But she wasn't giving up. The gal had spirit, you had to hand it to her. She was still trying to shout his name; she could see him—why couldn't he see her?

"Tony!"

Again it was no use. Try as she might, she couldn't yell any louder. The idea occurred to her—maybe if the porter, her friend Gus, tried. They knew each other well enough by now. She didn't know how she would have managed without Gus. "Yes, ma'am," he kept saying, and she was starting to feel like Vivien Leigh. Now, if he would only say "Yes, ma'am" one more time.

"Will you yell to him, please, Gus?" she said. "I'm sorry, but—"

"Yes, ma'am." And Gus let loose, booming in that rich Negro baritone that spoke of a heritage of suffering, life down on the Sewanee. "Tony!" he shouted. "Tony!"

This time Tony couldn't miss. He got an immediate directional fix and headed over, spotting the hefty black man calling his name, and next to him Francine, waving. When he reached her, they embraced, and for an irrepressible instant as Tony looked at Gus out of the corner of his eye, the silly thought entered his mind that Francine had left her husband and run away with a black man, who was the true father of her child. Now that would have been a movie, Paul Robeson and Betty Grable, but this was 1946, and they weren't making movies like that. For what it's worth, they're still not making them today. Anyway, the black man was wearing the uniform of a porter, a fact which in cinematic terms ruled him out of any serious consideration.

They exchanged further embraces and began to walk. Oh, and he almost forgot, reaching into his pocket and handing her a cracker.

"Here, take this," he said.

"A cracker?" She stared at him, her stomach upset enough without the practical jokes. Hadn't she already thrown up twice today, once the scrambled eggs and then the potato salad—and now a cracker? "Tony, a cracker? I ask for sympathy and you hand me a lousy cracker—"

"It's not a cracker. It's a saltine."

They were bumping into people as they walked, which jostled her tummy even more, causing tight wrinkles to form at the corners of her mouth. She wasn't quite turning green, but her natural curiosity made her wonder what was behind the idea of the cracker. Maybe it was some new religious order, an act of faith she hadn't heard of.

"Eat it," he said. "It settles the stomach."

"It does?" She took a few more steps, not having much of an appetite, in truth. "I never heard that. Who told you that?"

"Dorothy," he said. Dorothy was his wife. "Who do you think? We've got a baker's half-dozen at home."

"Crackers?"

"Kids."

He dug into his pocket and handed her a card, adding, "And she said to give you this. It's the name of her baby doctor. And she said to tell you not to worry. Almost everybody gets morning sickness. Some people also get it in the afternoon. A few people—and here's where you come in—even get it at showtime."

"Just lucky, I guess," she said. "I get it around the clock."

"She ain't lying," chimed in Gus. "She been awful sick, Tony."

They had almost forgotten about Gus, but there he was, walking alongside them, carrying her bags like a great bison. "She ain't lying, Tony."

Only his closest white friends called him Tony, and Tony said, "You can call me Mr. Harwell. My car's parked over here."

As they walked, a steady burning resentment built up in Gus. He wondered what on God's green earth made white folks so cruel, and if this had been his movie, he might have kicked some ass. But he was just a walk-on, paid by the day, and he needed the money. If he lost this job, his wife would kill him. So he kept his head down meekly and didn't say anything, didn't even listen to the rest of their conversation. He had already spoken his line.

"You'll be sick another month or so," Tony told her.

"Dorothy says it usually ends about the third month, and then——"

"Oh, God, no. What comes next?" She was afraid to hear. "Give me another cracker."

"Then you'll be on cloud nine," he said. "I remember the first time, Dorothy painted the house. The second time, she wallpapered it. The third time——"

"The third time she ate it." She couldn't resist, ever the wisecracker—and speaking of crackers, she was beginning to feel better already.

"Funny," Tony said. "You laugh now. You'll see. In a couple of weeks, you'll be itching to get to work."

"I'm itching now," she said. "I've gotta make some money."

"In your condition?"

"Especially in my condition."

As long as it didn't involve bouncing around in the back of a bus, she didn't see why not. There were all kinds of new horizons in New York, which was why she had chosen it. She could do radio commercials, for example. Once she got her doctor's permission, there were any number of things.

Chapter 2

THE FIRST TIME JOHNNY BOYLE MET BERNICE Thomas was at a party at the Sherman Hotel. Francine had gone back to New York that morning, and Paul had put in several calls to Chicago friends of his, people in the business of knowing.

"Any good singers around?" he asked.

The young lady one friend came up with was blond, rather on the chesty side and spicy. She wanted to meet Johnny, but for most of the evening he was unavailable, either sulking up in his room or over in the corner, worried about Francine. Bernice, too, was kept occupied, over by the punch bowl. Guys kept coming up.

"Hi, I'm Jerry. Wanna see my flute?"

Lines like that. But the best line was Boyle's, as usual. He had been eying Bernice, and now he finally got up off his duff and sauntered over on the slim pretense of getting refreshment in his cup. He didn't say anything at first, just ignoring her while he helped himself. He was reaching for the Ritz crackers, and filled with self-pity, and she seemed to understand this. She felt an urge to mother him. Certainly she meant no harm.

"I understand you're Johnny Doyle," she said.

"Yeah? Who says?"

He was biting a smoked herring, and she didn't quite know how to take him.

"Why, everybody," she said.

"Yeah? That ain't what they say about you," he said, that wicked gleam around his mouth shining on her like an oasis in the desert. She had no idea what he was getting at, but then, again, maybe she did.

"What's that?" she said.

"They say you dip faster than the cheese."

To his surprise, she smiled and stuck her finger in the cheese and proceeded to lick it. It was an auspicious meeting of the minds, but unfortunately it was all downhill from there. Bernice could do it all except sing.

A series of progressively dismal gigs now follows, increasing hints of rot and decay that are difficult to ignore ... *Johnny Doyle Orchestra, Three Week Engagement, Featuring Bernice Thomas*. In signs to come, her name disappeared altogether, but the band fared no better. Such few people dancing ... *Johnny Doyle, Limited Engagement* ... and even fewer people to be seen. In no time, the marquee will read *Closed,* and rain is falling, dripping forlornly from the sign. The band plays "Love for Sale" at the same time Bernice sings "This Can't Be Love," and even she begins to realize they're in trouble.

In the meantime, contrast that with Francine's mellifluous vocal stylings back in New York, where she's making demo recordings three times a week, singing not as herself but as others, anybody the occasion might call for. One day she's Helen O'Connell, another day Peggy Lee or Anita O'Day, and so on. It's all a part of the publishing game, selling songs to the stars. Someone like Peggy Lee, for example, who might get literally hundreds of song submissions in a single week—she couldn't possibly listen to them all, but she might listen to those featuring herself as vocalist—not really herself, of course, but someone who could mimic her with a little class. If she didn't like the sound of her own voice to start with or if the impersonation wasn't flattering, you were in trouble, and that's why the singer who could cut a good demo was worth her weight in gold. Thanks to her, the biggest names in the business could hear how a song would sound in advance of recording it, and the resultant time saved was easily worth a small token of appreciation to the girl responsible. In fact, many of the girls responsible went on to become stars in their own right in the not-too-distant future.

On the third Friday after her return to New York, Francine and Tony Harwell walked into a glass-enclosed booth adjoining a modern sound studio in downtown Manhattan, and several men got to their feet. One of them had red hair and introduced himself as Mr. Lord, extending to Francine a hand that held a piece of sheet music.

"Gentlemen, Francine Evans," Tony Harwell said. "The one you've all been hearing about."

They had heard good things about her and were anxious to shake hands. They were even more anxious to hear her sing. "Nice to meet you, Francine," said Mr. Lord. "He tell you what we want you to do? Or rather, who?"

"Bob Eberly?" she said, taking a wild stab.

"Jo Stafford. You can do Jo Stafford?"

"Sure. Jo Stafford . . . Jo Stafford . . . just a minute," she said and took a couple of steps to the corner, appearing in deep concentration.

"How much time does she need?" Mr. Lord asked Tony.

To which Tony replied, "Ask her yourself," because just then she rejoined them.

"I've got her," she said triumphantly, and a sigh of relief and wonder came over them all. A minute later she was at the studio mike, and an hour later she was on her way home. Not a bad day's work.

Chapter 3

HOME, YES. SOMETHING MODEST ON THE WEST SIDE, a one-bedroom with lots of glass and hardwood floors, solid workmanship in need only of personality and a little honest scrubbing, both of which Francine was eager to provide in abundance.

One afternoon like any other, as the sun was setting through the window of the bedroom, Francine was hammering hell out of the wall, driving in a heavy nail, perched on a stepladder secured by Ellen Flanery. They both wore carpenter's overalls, and Francine spoke with nails between her teeth.

"This should hold," she said.

"Unless the building falls," said Ellen, pricking up her ears as if she heard something in the next room. It seemed to her she heard a key turn in the door, but then Francine began to hammer anew in search of the perfect stroke.

CUT TO living room, what Ellen heard . . . a couple of suitcases being placed on the threshold of the apartment, and Johnny coming in the front door, admitted silently by the landlady, who now conspires with him to keep his arrival a surprise. He gives her a nod and a wink as she leaves and shuts the door softly, and now he turns to survey the apartment, the evidence of Francine's handiwork everywhere—odds and ends, mementoes, paint rollers and books, whole stacks of them. It's just as he always imagined how a newlywed's first place should look.

The hammering continuing, Johnny picks up a couple of books, curious to see what sort of things she's reading. He never knew her to be such a big reader. CLOSE ON book titles . . . *The Albert Einstein Story, Science for Mankind, History of the Byzantine Empire,* light stuff like that. Her physical condition had made her ambitious; here were all the books she'd been meaning to read over the years and had never gotten around to. Now, when the hammering stopped, he heard her voice from the next room.

"There," he heard her say with ringing satisfaction. "Finally. Let's see what that does for us . . ."

With Ellen's help, she was trying to hang a wall mirror, the mirror precariously balanced in her grasp, as a voice behind her and his image in the reflecting glass at the same time gave her a shock—

"Francine, it ain't straight."

The mirror dropped straight down the wall and shattered in a thousand pieces, as she turned, looked at him, nails still in her mouth . . . FADE OUT.

147

A day or so later the mirror-hanging process was repeated, and this time it was Boyle who tried his luck. For a guy who played sax with either hand tied behind his back, he was all thumbs as he raised a new mirror while Francine insisted on helping. That meant climbing the ladder with him where only one was meant to tread and lending him assistance despite his protests. Before it was all over, it was like the Three Stooges gouging each other.

"For chrissake, Francine, whadda you think you're doing?" he said. "You fall off here, you're gonna break like Humpty-Dumpty. You're making me nervous."

But he needed her help. "You want me to let go?" she said.

"What? You want me to hurt myself? Hang on."

Onward together, backward never . . . later, their reflections in the mirror after a job well done, late afternoon, shadows falling, as they lay on the bed, arm in arm.

Still later, it was dusk, the darkness of twilight settling on them as the two of them sat in the living room in a slipcovered armchair, though Francine always said she detested slipcovered furniture . . . "I mean, what are they saving it for?" . . . but now that she had furniture of her own, she had yet to get around to taking off the covers. What was she saving it for? There were coffee cups, half filled, in front of them. Johnny was smoking. Her head was on his arm. There was silence while she nestled closer, and how long they had been like this was anybody's guess. "Mmm," was all she said.

Johnny had already spoken his piece. He had talked about the band, the difficulties, the fiascos, but hadn't mentioned Bernice until she said, "How'd the singer work out?"

He changed the subject, running a hand over her

head and smoothing a bump he didn't recall. "You got a bump on your head?" he said.

"It's always been there."

"Oh. It just felt different." He gave a sigh, as if he held the burdens of the whole world on his shoulders, the kind of pretentious sigh only the young can get away with. "It's OK," he said, "I got a hole in mine."

They were back to square one, and she wanted to comfort him but knew better. He was in no mood for anything but the gloomy side.

"I never wanted a band in the first place," he said. "All I ever wanted to do was play music. You're right. Just goes to prove I'm not cut out for the band business—we get to Detroit and the guy takes one look at us and says we got too many musicians. It dawns on me he hates musicians, and this bastard's in charge of my destiny, right? He says, 'Why should I pay sixteen guys when the people can dance to twelve?' How can you argue with that? It's taken this s.o.b. ten years to come to this brilliant deduction. Why pay sixteen when twelve can play as loud? Why pay twelve guys when you can get a tenor band with six or seven poor slobs? Pretty soon you've got yourself a trio, then a folk singer on stage with amplified banjo—" He caught his breath. "That's the way we're headed. All the latest trends indicate—"

"You didn't have time, Johnny," she said, being the realist. "They weren't your musicians, they were Frankie's. You tried to change things, but if you had your own guys—maybe sometime in the future—"

"What future? The kind of future like Paul Wilson?" he said. "He thinks he can build a band with those characters. I wouldn't hire them to build a bandstand."

"So, you're right," she said, getting to her feet, not about to argue with him. A persecuted man is always right. "What future? The only solution now is to kill

149

yourself—I'll bring you the dust mop and you can stick your face in it. As for me—"

She was heading for the bedroom.

"Where're you going?" he called after her.

She turned in the doorway. It was too early for bed, but she'd rather wait for it to get dark than listen to this. "This is the bedroom," she said matter-of-factly. "Some of us have to get up in the morning to go to work."

Boyle was slow to understand. "No, I don't," he said. "I ain't gotta be anywhere tomorrow."

"Oh, good. Then you can come with me."

While he mulled over that, she retired and closed the door. She hadn't had the chance to tell him she was working—either that, or she hadn't had the heart. He looked so cute when he was quiet and discouraged.

Chapter 4

THEY HAD THEIR FIRST MAJOR FIGHT THE NEXT day—in the recording studio at the boom microphone. Francine was standing there with Mr. Lord and the studio band leader, conferring with them about the day's sheet music, a tune she was certain she wasn't seeing for the first time.

"Hey, this looks familiar."

"Yeah, it's the same song you did last for Stafford," said Mr. Lord, "but she passed on it. We're thinking of Teresa Brewer this time—"

"Teresa Brewer?" she said, never failing to be surprised by things in this business. "Whadda they think I am—a female impersonator?"

It was the last lighthearted line of the day. She spotted someone and waved; the others turned to see that Johnny Boyle had just come into the observation booth with Tony Harwell. No one knew what either of them was doing there, so she must have invited them. Frankly, she had asked them to come in hopes that they would learn to like each other. As I've said, Francine had one blind spot, and that was JB. She thought in time he would grow on everybody the way he had grown on her, and for the time being, trapped behind soundproof glass, Boyle did have an underrated cuteness, the fuzziness of a small wild creature. He looked docile and clearly delighted with the whole setup, making faces at the spectators. His sharp little eyes devoured the shiny equipment, and he seemed mesmerized, waving back.

"That's my husband," she told them proudly. "You oughtta hear him play sometime. He's terrific." She waved at him again, a little I-love-you-too wave that embarrassed everyone.

"Never mind that. Can you do Teresa Brewer?" they said.

"Whadda you think I've been working for all these years?" she shot back. Musicians rented by the hour were standing around, playing with themselves, and it was up to her. "Let's get started," she said.

In the meantime one of the studio musicians passing near the observation booth heard a knock on the window and glanced up to see Johnny Boyle gesturing to him in an importuning way. As fate would have it, the musician himself was a saxophonist, and in the commonplace use of signs known only to members of that strange esoteric sect, Boyle was merely indicating for the man to hold up his sheet music to the glass so he could get a look at it. It was an easily granted request, but it wasn't the request so much as Boyle's superior attitude that rankled the man, and he had his little fun by holding up the music all right but turning it upside down. What he couldn't know was that Boyle had long ago learned to read this brand of upside-down sheet music when, as a deeply religious lad in one of the bio-pic's earliest scenes, he mastered the fine art of leaning out of the choir loft to drool at the attractive organist below. In the process of staring at her bosom, he learned to read the music sheet she was using, which, from where he stood, was upside down. Later, the same woman volunteered to teach him other up-side-down things.

Now he tried to sit down and be still but found that he couldn't. Even when the musician withdrew the music, Johnny was left with an itch to become involved in today's affair, an idea which even he knew was dangerous. He told himself to be calm, and wondered why he should be the one to be nervous. After all, it wasn't his session, it was hers.

Tony Harwell noticed him pacing the floor and considered doing the young war vet a favor. "Would you like to record here sometime, Boyle?"

"Oh, gee, Mr. Harwell, that'd be swell!" Dick Powell's eyes got big, but Boyle stood at the glass, just tapping his fingers. Tony decided against making the offer, and Boyle wiped his hands on his pants. His palms were clammy. In the next room they were almost set.

"This isn't just a run-through, right?" Johnny asked him. "She's gonna record this and it ain't gonna sound bad—"

Tony reassured him. "It's not gonna sound bad. It'll be all right."

"All right? It's gotta be better than all right," Johnny said, the old familiar crimson creeping into his face. You could almost hear the fuse blow before he did it, 10-9-8-7 . . . going, going, gone. "How do I get in there?" he suddenly said, and there was no stopping him now. "I gotta tell her something—"

Tony saw what he had in mind and tried to stop

152

him. "Boyle, they're almost ready to record. Wait a minute!"

Francine was at the mike, almost ready to begin, when she saw the flurry of activity in the observation room, saw Tony almost crack the glass trying to get her attention. Accordingly she held things up, took another breath to get ready and stepped back from the mike just as the studio door opened and Johnny came in, heading straight for her, notwithstanding the voice from the control room.

"This is a recording session," announced the voice, not recognizing the intruder.

She made the identification into the mike. "It's my husband," she said, hoping that would put everyone at ease, but it didn't work in her own case. She herself wasn't at all clear about what he might have up his sleeve, and she turned just as he arrived, trying to keep one hand over the microphone to prevent their words from being saved for posterity.

"Johnny—"

He hadn't come for small talk. His mind was on the music, immediately pointing to her copy of the arrangement. "Look at this here," he said, wanting to help, and in a way she was truly touched, but then she wasn't the one paying for the overhead. He went on, picking out the parts he thought could stand some real improvement. "I was just looking at the sax player's part, and some of this is pretty ridiculous. I got a couple of ideas—"

Maybe she was partially guilty for not having explained things sufficiently at breakfast. "Johnny, it's just a demo," she said.

"Yeah, but—" He paused, eyes serious. "It's just a demo? But that's why it's even more important. This is what people are gonna hear, they're gonna know it's you. It's gotta put your name in people's heads. Just lemme play sax for you, I'll back you up—"

153

And before she could object, he stepped over a couple of rows to borrow a saxophone from the same musician who had showed him the music through the glass. The latter was at first extremely reluctant to give up his horn, but Boyle made him see the light.

"Give me your sax. I'm her husband."

It was an old playground tactic, and the sax player yielded. "It's a shit song, anyway," he said, looking on the bright side.

Meanwhile, as might be expected, the place was getting steamed, including Mr. Lord and especially Tony Harwell. Francine realized all this, but Boyle was totally unaware of the effect he was having, standing off to one side of the mike and raising the sax, giving his chops a quick workout.

She motioned for everyone to stay cool and said, "I think we'll be all right."

That was wishful thinking. Not only did Boyle want to play, he wanted to lead the band, rubbing salt in the guys' wounds by leading them in with a quick intro: "On three—one—two—three—"

The guys held back, waiting to watch him make an ass of himself. When he didn't, they liked what they heard, and he told them to try again. He raised his hand. "All right—" He blew the opening few bars, as if getting warmed up, showing off for good cause. "Take it from the top," he said, and they did.

Boyle himself lengthened the lead-in, playing around the band, dropping in, dropping out. It sounded marvelous. Everything was prepared for her. It was good, it was terrific—that is, until Francine stepped up to the mike and started to sing like Teresa Brewer.

For a minute Boyle didn't even notice, wrapped up in his own performance and the band, but then he listened, and he couldn't believe what he was hearing. It wasn't possible—it was heresy. What had happened to the one and only Francine Evans and her honey-smooth pipes? This sounded more like Teresa Brewer, for crying out loud.

He lowered the sax, glaring at everyone. But they ignored him. His own wife ignored him, the band ignored his hand signals to stop playing, and across the room Tony Harwell despised him and ignored him, also. He had never felt like such an idiot, standing in the middle of a recording studio while his wife sang like Teresa Brewer and people looked through him like he wasn't there. It didn't take him long to head for the door. He thought at least she would make eye contact with him, but when she made a point of looking the other way, he couldn't contain himself, red light or no red light.

"You sound like Teresa Brewer!" he shouted at her. "What the hell did they do to you?"

In a series of heavy groans, the band died down, and the voice from the control room was back. "This is a recording session. Get him out of here."

She had taken his side up till now, but there were limits even to her patience, and he had just committed the biggest sin of all in her book, the sin of being unprofessional in his conduct. She could rationalize away almost anything but that.

"Johnny, for the love of Christ, can't you see what we're doing here, you . . . you . . ." She couldn't think of the word. "We're making a Teresa Brewer demo—can't you understand that? I'm supposed to sound like her . . ."

Boyle just stood there, lacking any sense of cohesion, as she lambasted him again. "I didn't tell you 'cause I wanted to surprise you. I've got her voice down pretty good . . . I've got all their voices down pretty good, and . . . Anyway, it's still no excuse for you to come in here and—"

Tony Harwell felt he could be of some use in a situation like this, and he got up to show Boyle the door.

"That's right, Boyle," he said. "I'll explain it all to you later. Come on."

But Johnny shook off his hand, yelled back at her. "You're making demos for other people! That's worse than going backwards—I did that in high school. What the hell you call that? It's chickenshit. They oughtta be making demos for you to sing, not the other way round—What the hell's this, an agent? You call him an agent?"

With a single punch he knocked Tony to one side and brushed his hands, a move they're still talking about in industry circles. Tony was out of action, but there were plenty of others where he came from. Boyle couldn't take them all, and he knew it, so he backed slowly toward the door, keeping his eyes on all approaches.

"You're not supposed to be working," he said to her, like Cagney being backed into a corner. They didn't have him as long as he kept his wits about him. He tossed back a strand of hair dangling over his forehead; beads of sweat served to inform others, Come no closer, you bastards. "Anyway, I thought you were supposed to be sick," he said to her. "You got no business working. C'mon, let's go."

"Johnny, wait'll I'm finished!" she screamed at him, and things were getting serious. Serious questions about their compatibility were raised by band members, most of whom had successfully survived several marriages and recognized the little warning signs involved. Gritting one's teeth the way Francine was doing it was one of these. "Get out of here, Johnny. Wait'll I'm finished, or I'm gonna have the baby on the floor. I'll see you later."

"No, you'll see me now," he said, standing firm. " 'Cause I ain't leaving."

All this time Mr. Lord had not been heard from. Where was Mr. Lord? He had stepped next door to

156

have a cup of coffee but now appeared in the control room, in a no-nonsense mood, looking through the glass in an official capacity, as Francine went over to where Johnny was, intent on talking this thing out.

Mr. Lord seized the microphone and said, "Evans, if you leave this room, you're fired."

She went out anyway. If he wanted to fire her, he could do as he liked. There were certain things she and Johnny had to settle before they went any further, and one of them was who was going to bring home the bacon in a steady way.

Chapter 5

JOHNNY BOYLE HAD VOLUNTEERED TO BRING HOME the bacon, but it wasn't that simple. He would have to wait in line like the others.

CLOSE ON marbled glass door, *American Federation of Musicians, Local 802,* as Johnny opened it and headed inside, a union hiring hall, milling musicians out of work, loitering and looking jaded, conversing, passing bottles . . . a subculture all their own, Johnny's entry into it hardly making a ripple except for the flowers he carried, a small bouquet. Why flowers? Well, contrary to some semisarcastic suggestions from his fellows, they were meant for no one's funeral, not even the death knell of the big bands in general, eight of whom—count them, eight of the biggest—Benny Goodman, Harry James, Tommy Dorsey, Benny Carter, Jack Teagarden, Les Brown, Woody Herman and Ina Ray Hutton—would all throw in the towel in a matter of weeks. No, Boyle had no time to concern himself with that, nor tears for the predicaments of others. Pundits could debate from now till eternity the reasons for the big bands' demise, but individuals must live in the world they find and not pause unduly to reflect. That was why Boyle was carrying the flowers, just a little something that set him apart from the rest of them and served notice in his own way that the world had yet to hear the last of him.

He seemed to know his way around. He ultimately arrived at the desk of a stout lady who was in charge of several matters at once, speaking with authority into the phone and barely taking notice of him as he took a seat on the edge of her desk, the spot already polished clean from the trousers of others who from time to time had had the same notion—to get on Annie's good side. As she hung up, she found herself looking into his smiling face. She had seen a lot of faces over the years but could not recall a more counterfeit mouth than his. It had to be counterfeit, she thought. No one had such a smile outside the movies.

"Hi ya, Annie, what's new?" he said. "Whadda you got for me today? Remember me?"

She saw so many guys. "Refresh my memory," she said.

"I'm the one who asked you to run away with me day before yesterday."

She couldn't remember the day before yesterday. She could hardly remember this morning when two foul-smelling thugs had followed her from the subway train, repeating obscenities. By the time she saw a cop, she had overheard enough of their conversation to know she was in no danger. They were just musicians, desperate and out of work. Thank God for her knowledge of musical terms, she thought, as she said hello to the cop and kept walking. The town was full of hungry musicians, and here was another.

"I thought you looked familiar," she said.

He smiled and she smiled, and the phone rang again. She didn't pick up the receiver at once, and Boyle knew he didn't have more than a second to make his pitch. The phone still rang, and he still hadn't spoken. Then he blurted, "How many times I gotta tell you— it's a close-kept secret, but you're looking at the Sound of the Fifties. You can be my agent if you want, ten percent straight across the board——"

Nix. She had thought somehow he would come up with something more original than that. Her hand reached for the telephone and she shook her head. "Don't you ever give up?" she said.

She picked up the phone, looked at him as if he should have known it was hopeless. Didn't he know that was the consensus around here? Indeed he did, and he started to walk away, pausing just long enough to recall the flowers he had brought. There was a small vase on her desk with a two-day-old bouquet that was remarkably similar to the one he was carrying, and he replaced the old with the new. By now Annie wasn't even looking, but as he left, he said anyway, "If you get any hot tips——"

She wasn't hearing him too well either, with one ear to the phone. She stuck a finger in her ear and said "What?"

"I said, 'If you get any hot tips——' "

She nodded and went back to the phone. Seldom had his charm failed him so completely. He was feeling in the dumps, and he decided to give the place one last try.

He wound up in the vicinity of a cluster of other down-and-out prodigies gone to pot. Together they looked on as the hiring boss came out of a back room in shirt-sleeves and sweaty suspenders, but in one hand he clutched hope. He had a couple of jobs.

"Alvino Rey needs a bass man in the worst way, upstate," he barked. "We got anybody here? No jokers, no jive—salary negotiable. Own transportation. Skidmore Girls' College tomorrow night."

159

That, as expected, brought a flurry of inquiries, in the main pertaining to suggested sexual perversions known to be popular among college coeds, in turn prompting the white man to add judiciously, "Whites only."

A colored voice came over Johnny's shoulder: "You full of shit, man."

The process continued, the world kept turning—but Johnny turned out of curiosity to see where the angry colored voice had come from, and he saw three of them standing together, one of them no stranger. Boyle had always prided himself on his ability to tell colored people apart, but this one had him stumped. Who was that guy, and where had he seen him before? Then he remembered, and he could have kicked himself. Of course, Cecil Baby, that was his name . . . Cecil Powell, who used to work week nights at the Palm Club in Brooklyn.

He was still looking him over, and now Cecil stared back, having the same problem—remembering who Boyle was. But then something clicked and the little lights came on. Cecil smiled. "Hey!" he said.

"Cecil—"

Johnny went toward the group and shook hands with Cecil, wondering to himself why colored people always seemed to be more numerous than they really were. Three of them seemed like six, six of them seemed like twelve, and so forth; it was possible to be surrounded by one colored person. He didn't know why this was so. He kept smiling as Cecil offered him a pocket flask.

"This is Johnny," Cecil told his pals. "Johnny Boyle, right? Remember me?"

"You look different in the light," Johnny said.

"I just wish I did. Well, hey, this is Kenny Young, Matthew Sanders—friends of mine. What're you doin'?"

160

"I don't know. Lookin'."

"Ain't we all? Lookin' for money—"

"You can have the money. I'm lookin' for music," Johnny said.

That was an odd thing for a white man to say, and Cecil did a quick reappraisal, deciding the young man was on the level. Johnny had always struck him as a little different, distant from other white people, and he took that as a good sign. What he failed to understand was that Johnny was equally distant from all people, regardless of race. They were all just human beings as far as Johnny was concerned, and in that sense he seemed remarkably free of prejudice.

"So you still dig music?" Cecil said.

"Always."

"You still dig music when there ain't no money— that's good," Cecil said, " 'cause there's lots of music but not much of the other."

"Amen, brother," said his friends.

"Amen," said Johnny, and it was apparent Cecil had uttered a great truth.

They all looked at each other, nodding, and Johnny looked back at the hiring director, the shop foreman, the plantation boss, the sweating man in the suspenders who held aloft another recent opening. "Roxy Burlesque on Forty-second Street," said the man. "It's non-union, so any of you bastards who go over there, sneak in the back. I have no respect for anyone who would take this job."

Johnny turned back to the blacks. "So what're you guys doing? You got something goin' on? I ain't heard no offers yet, so maybe you can't let white cats in on it."

"It ain't much, just a gig, man," Cecil said.

"Where, in Harlem?"

Cecil nodded. "You know Minton's Playhouse?"

"The 'Birthplace of Bop.' Sure, I know it."

"It's just up the street from Minton's."

Having said that, Cecil and the guys seemed ready to hit the road, Cecil reaching in his pocket and coming up with a matchbook, handing it to Johnny. The name on the matchbook was the Club 88. Later on it would become the Rocket 88, when the famous Oldsmobile appeared.

"Come on up sometime," Cecil said, as he turned to leave. "We're there till four in the morning. You can sit in—get some kicks—Sonny Stitt, Gene Ammons, all them cats hang around."

Johnny didn't take much convincing. As he watched them walk off, he had half a mind to follow. "Where're you going now?" he called after them.

Cecil turned, walking backward. "You mean right now?" he said.

"Yeah. Why don't I come with you now?" Johnny suggested. "You going to Harlem?"

"No. We're going to Macy's, the record department."

Johnny was caught flat-footed and decided for the time being to stay where he was and not appear so anxious. "Oh, good," he said. "Then I'll see you tonight."

He looked after them as they made their way through the crowd, black in their baggy suits, with straightened hair and smelling of rose water. How he wished he were colored—the way they could disappear in black ponds and come up only when they pleased. If only his hands were black—with a gold saxophone, he could be the kingfish of the world. . . .

His daydream was interrupted by the hiring boss's raising his voice again, with yet another opportunity that seemed too real to be true. "Legion Hall on Long Island needs somebody to blow trumpet at sunset," said the man. "Any of you guys patriotic?"

162

Chapter 6

DAWN, A FEW DAYS LATER, AND FRANCINE TURNED off the water in the kitchen sink and listened to the faint sound of someone trying to turn a key in the front door without making any noise. The door opened and closed, and there followed the sound of light footsteps in the hall. Obviously the perpetrator's intentions were good, and only his timing was bad. He hadn't wished to disturb but had disturbed already. She hadn't slept all night, the sun was already up, and he was just now home. One followed the other.

She waited for a moment, let him take another step or two before she spoiled his little game. Soap was dripping off her fingers.

"It's all right," she said just loud enough for her anger to register. "I'm up."

Her hair was in a net, but out of habit she primped it all the same. There were soapsuds over her ear when he poked his head around the door and made a point of winding his watch, presumably slow.

"It's seven o'clock here," he said.

"What was it in Africa?" she said.

He came over to give her a kiss, smooching her wetly as if to apologize, putting his arms around her waist, but she was having none of it. This made three nights in a row.

"What was it where you were?" she said.

"A little later." He murmured semiromantically, vodka on his breath, "Hi, doll. Always good to get home—home, sweet home—"

He was really full of it this morning, she thought. "Where'd you go?" she said.

"Just some guys."

"What guys? The guys from—"

"No, you don't know these guys."

"I don't know any of them. You're right."

They didn't know the same people any more, and whose fault was that? She didn't know, but was fuming all the same, longing for the days when they used to have silly fights and it was someone's fault. Now all he did was talk about himself among strangers, and she did the same, and in the telling it became painfully clear that the two of them were the real strangers—to each other.

"What's this?" he said, investigating what she was cooking for breakfast, sniffing the pans on the stove.

"Get away from there," she said, when he lifted one too many lids to suit her. "Stay out of that."

"What're you trying to do, cook?"

And so forth. That's the way it seemed to go lately. "Sometimes you really suck the hose, Johnny," she said. "Johnny, I swear—get out of here before I—"

That was a new one on him, and he thought he'd heard them all. "The what—?" he said. "Suck what?"

"Suck the hose!" she shouted. "Suck the goddamn hose! Why didn't you call last night? You could have called! Don't you remember when you were kids, there was always one kid who sucked the hose to get the water out? Well, that's you. All you do is suck, you don't give! Damn it, Johnny, I had a bad night last night—"

He was sorry to hear that, if, in fact, he heard it at all. He was speaking roughly at the same time. "That makes me a sucker," he said.

"No, I'm the sucker," she said, flinging a wet dishrag. "So where'd you go?"

He reached in his pocket, took out a book of matches and dropped it into a large brandy snifter which already contained a sizable number of them. The mere act, the way he did it, served as an invitation to fight.

"I brought you a couple of matchbooks for your collection," he said.

"Keep your goddamn matches!"

And she knocked the collection over, spilling the brandy snifter and its contents all over the floor, while, as if on cue, the coffeepot on the stove boiled over, sending coffee running over the grill and sizzling on the electric burner. She was sorry, but she found some satisfaction in the event because it matched her mood perfectly, the two of them glaring at one another while neither made a move to rescue the pot.

"What're you waiting for?" she said with a smile, and in that moment she knew he thought she was crazy, and it gave her pleasure. She said, "Why don't you do something? Take it off. I gotta do everything around here?" Her smile frightened him.

With elaborate chivalry he removed the coffeepot, and now there were two of them with kindly smiles. "Of course," he said. "Anything else I can do for you? As long as I'm up, I think I'll put on some music."

"Oh, no, you don't. I'll play the music around here," she said, backing up to block the door. "It's my record player."

"Oh, it's your record player? Well, might I request a song?"

"It's my record player," she said.

He thought seriously of removing her by force but had the sense instead to sit down and look bored, as if the discussion was over as far as he was concerned. He opened yesterday's sports pages and noted where the Tribe had just been in town for a twin bill and the Bums had clobbered the Bucs, and though ordinarily not a fan, he was seen to read such items voraciously. Out of the corner of his eye, he saw her disappear into the living room and yelled after her, "Yeah, well, put

165

on one of your demos, or I'm gonna break your legs."

Almost at once she was back in the doorway. His back to her, he couldn't see the sarcastic grin on her face and the red vinyl demo record she was holding in one hand. She sounded eager to please, saying, "Put it on, you said? My demo record?"

"You heard me," he said without looking up. "Teresa Brewer's my favorite."

That's all she wanted to hear. Without a moment's delay, she nonchalantly laid the red disc on the electric burner where the coffeepot had been and then calmly went about her kitchen chores, such as pouring him a cup of sticky coffee with half the sugarbowl dumped in.

"Sugar, sugar?"

"I don't hear it," he said, meaning the record.

"You will," she said, and her nose was sniffing it already.

"What's that stink?" he said.

"Oh, just my famous pancakes."

"Holy Mother! Christ!"

And he was up in a flash, a blur, lunging from his chair to the stove, seizing the record from atop the electric burner where it had so unceremoniously began to dissolve. Melted, hot and smoking, it fell to the floor, and he began to stomp the edges.

"That's your record!" he hollered, surprisingly enough coming to her defense.

But she motioned very coolly for him to get out of the way and proceeded to pour the coffee from the coffeepot all over the place, effectively dousing the record along with everything else.

"I've got a whole box," she said, continuing to pour. She poured coffee on the table, over the sports section, coffee everywhere, and it was at this point that Boyle decided he'd seen enough and left.

"That's it—that's all it took. You're crazy! I'm leaving."

She sat down in a wet chair and recited a joke she'd heard some years ago, maybe even when she was a kid—she couldn't remember now. She said, "Know what time it is when Mama Bear sits in your chair?"

There was no answer other than the sound of his feet heading back toward the front door, and, knowing him, she doubted whether he could have guessed right in a million years.

"Time to get a new chair," she said, as the front door slammed.

Chapter 7

FRANCINE AT THE MIKE OF THE RECORDING STUDIO had become a familiar sight by now, but these days she was tummified around the middle. She was starting to bulge prominently, and the rogues in the band remarked that it wouldn't be long now, as Mr. Lord handed her a nice new song to sing, which was hardly new in any event. But first things first. . . . There was the matter of her appearance, her eyes a little washed out around the rims, a touch of redness remaining. What a jive artist Boyle was. Who else would make a pregnant woman cry?

"You all right?" said Mr. Lord, perhaps even caring. "What'd you have, a rough night?"

"No, I'm fine," she said, appreciating his concern but not regarding him as anyone she would care to have a chat with. She was paid for singing, and that was what she was here for. Just give her the music, and she'd take it from there. But something about this tune reminded her of . . . but that was impossible. This one had a calypso beat. All the same: "This looks like—"

Mr. Lord nodded to confirm her worst suspicions, and she sighed. Of all the——! "It's the same song," he said. "Teresa Brewer didn't go for it. This time we're shooting for Martha Tilton."

"Why not just shoot her and get it over with?" she said, looking at the piece of music that looked nothing like itself, at least the way it had been originally. Jo Stafford, Teresa Brewer, Martha Tilton . . . who would it be next? They had already turned it into calypso. Later, another gimmick. That's the way these people thought. They never gave up and said the truth, that maybe it was just a lousy song to start with and all the cosmetic changes in the world wouldn't put it in the Hit Parade. It was like a man——you could change this and that about him, hope for the best, but sooner or later you came to the realization that he was as he was because of what was on the inside and you couldn't reach that to change it. If you changed it, it would cease to be him at all, it would be someone else——like saying, "We like the song, but let's try it this time with a different melody." What song? There came a time when you had to say, "That's it," about men or songs, write them off like a bad debt. What was she saying, she thought. She had to write Johnny off? Never. She loved him just the way he was. But if she loved him the way he was, why was she so miserable that when she had walked in the studio this morning everyone had known the two of them had been at it again, fighting?

These were hard questions, but they were none of Mr. Lord's concern. He saw her staring blankly at the sheet music and just assumed she was studying it when her eyes didn't blink. "OK, Evans?" he said.

"What?" she said, glancing up.

"How's your Martha Tilton?"

"My Martha Tilton's great," she said.

Some evenings, though, they were like any other

168

married couple, on those rare occasions when Johnny stayed home, usually because she asked him. She read a book; he played piano with his tie loosened, fancying himself Gershwin. When he did look up, it was in response to a question she might put to him on any number of theoretical subjects from A to Z.

One night she asked him, "You understand Einstein?"

"Sure," he said. "Don't you?"

"What's the essence of the theory of relativity? That light is curved?" she said, not expecting the mathematical answer. She would give him partial credit if he could put it into simple English. She already knew the correct answer, and so had something of an advantage.

"I used to know," he said after a long pause during which it seemed he wouldn't answer at all. Indeed, he showed some irritation with her choice of questions. She put her book aside and got up from the couch and came over, running a finger along the smooth cold piano.

"They say there's only five people in the world," she said, "only five people in the world who understand what he meant."

Boyle wasn't so sure. "The Japs understand," he said. Part of the reason he didn't care for this particular category of knowledge, was that he considered himself also a genius of sorts. His one sore point, she had always noticed, was whenever she brought up the subject of great men. Einstein particularly inflamed him. Abraham Lincoln was another.

She leaned against the piano, touched his hair. The notes he played reminded her of better times. Funny, the tricks the memory played. The mind of a human is so intricate and yet with such little capacity to remember bad times. Only the good bob to the top. It was that melody of his she had completely forgotten about since that night on the bus. Probably he had, too.

"Remember this?" he said.

"How could I forget? What was it we called it?"

He thought a minute. " 'New York,' " he said.

" 'New York'? Are you sure that was it?"

"Remember, we said we'd name it after the place where we were, and—"

"Oh, yeah," she remembered. "And I said one thing, and you said another."

"I said 'New York,' " he said.

" 'New York,' " she said with a trace of disappointment. "It sounded more romantic then. How about 'New York, New York'?"

Then he remembered, and his face was brighter for an instant, as he plunked the chords. "Yeah, that was it. 'New York, New York'—I hate it."

"You liked it then."

"It's derivative as hell," he said.

"Everything's derivative if you wanna be that way about it. There are just twelve notes. Some people say there's just seven jokes—"

"I'm number eight," he said and played something else, but by now she knew the chords and could play the song herself, and she vowed that she would. She would even add some words. With her propensity for poetry and human observation, that shouldn't be too difficult. She sat down beside him on the bench, letting her fingers follow his for a minute but finding that her fingers had a will of their own and longed for the old tunes.

"When you get right down to it," she said, "how about a little Harry James? I'll make it worth your while. You play your sax—"

"No, I don't want to play." It was just his sax he didn't want to play, that being a matter of principle. He didn't play music like this on his saxophone any more. But he didn't object to playing the piano, trading

170

song titles with her. "Harry James," he said. " 'You Made Me Love You' . . ."

He went a few bars, and then it was her turn. " 'Fools Rush In' " . . . and so forth.

" 'It's Funny to Everyone but Me,' " he cut in.

" 'You Don't Know What Love Is.' "

" 'I'll Get By,' " he said.

From the song titles, a bebop, jazzed version of "I'll Get By," Johnny on sax in the wee hours of a Harlem club. The music's hot, but everyone's cool. Being cool is the secret. Who's got the secret? The white guy might have the secret. Cecil Powell and friends are blowing, too, but the only white cat is something of a celebrity. *This* is the kind of sax he wants to play.

Johnny swooping, Johnny flying at the end of his rope, bebop man, hanging out, smoking dope—then catching a breath, lowering his sax, as someone yells out from the back, "Johnny—telephone!"

At first he doesn't want to leave the bandstand. Like, it's the middle of his thing, man. He's just going good, feeling like a tan man. Tin can, also ran, bed pan, Polish ham, Superman, Stan the Man—Kenton, not Musial.

"Who is it?"

"It's your wife."

He takes a step down, heading back to the pay phone, our eyes on him as he makes his way through the smoky club and encounters handshakes, black jive . . . if not the dozens, the half-dozens . . . a black woman going so far as to reach out and wrap an arm around his leg as he goes by, Johnny pausing to whisper something in her ear . . . a kiss . . . causing her to scream with laughter.

By the time he reaches the telephone, he has very little energy left. He picks up the phone and shuts the glass door, but there is no keeping the noise out. We can hear only the first few words . . .

"Hey, I was in the middle of a set."

Chapter 8

NIGHTS PASSED, AND ON THE NIGHTSTAND AT HOME A light still burned for him, though there wasn't much else that did. They read different magazines that weren't even current, and one night in bed she finally said it.

"Something's the matter."

Like a helium balloon, the words kind of floated to the ceiling and popped. There was a silence, and Boyle didn't take his eyes from his magazine, knowing nevertheless that things were altered somehow just because she had ventured to say it. He couldn't ignore the changing times, either, and he turned the page of the week-old copy of *Down Beat*.

"Yeah," he said.

"You know what it is?" she said, turning to look at him, her finger marking her place in the *Collier's*.

"No, I just know something's the matter. We gotta work out some things."

"What things?"

He turned another page, and a blurb about the Paul Wilson Orchestra caught his eye. The Paul Wilson Orchestra was appearing in Buffalo, had just closed its second week. No figures were given. He went to the next page, looked at a picture of a golden Conn trumpet with a New York mouthpiece.

"I don't know exactly," he said. "Some things. We gotta make some kind of compromise—"

"I thought that's what we did—when we got married, I mean."

"Oh, you feel compromised?"

"Slightly," she said. "When I'm in bed with a man, I generally feel compromised."

"Generally" meant more than one. He didn't like the word.

"Whadda you mean, 'generally'?"

"I mean, isn't that the idea? When you're married, you're naturally supposed to feel compromised—and that's the way I feel, naturally. I mean, it's normal."

"Just like pouring my coffee?" he said.

It was the line she had once said to him when they talked about the baby, but it hadn't come up in a long time. It turned out she didn't pour his coffee anyway. She just looked at him. "Maybe you shouldn't feel that way," he said. "Maybe I shouldn't, either."

"Maybe we shouldn't be married," she said, and the words were out of her mouth before she realized what she was saying. Even so, it was something that needed to be said, and she was confident, now that it was out in the open, that they would kiss and squeeze one another tight and say, "Don't ever say that again."

But Johnny's response was simply to roll over and cut the light, saying, "Maybe we're not. I'm gonna go check in the morning." He kissed her shoulder like he always did. "Goodnight," he said.

She was biting her lip less than a foot away from him, but there might as well have been the Royal Gorge separating them. She had the choice of looking at the wall or the back of his head. "Aren't you gonna say goodnight?" he said. So his eyes weren't closed, after all. He was probably thinking the same thing she was, only wanting her to be the one to do it, wanting to feel her arms engulf him and rock him like a baby.

Accordingly, she put her arms around him, struggled to pull him next to her, but by then it was apparent he was perfectly happy where he was. "Goodnight. I love you, Johnny," she said.

"I love you, too."

And he dropped back like a slippery whale into his former position, snoring almost as soon as his head hit the indentation in the pillow, his right ear finding its niche, and he looked just too comfy. There was also something in the tone of his voice she didn't like, any number of things recently, little things she had noticed. Some might have called them clues, and she certainly wasn't blind to the possibilities. It was just that she had always considered herself relatively liberal-minded and had vowed never to become the sort of accusing, suspicious wife in folklore; but now as she watched him lying there, that omniscient smirk he wore even in sleep, she had to ask herself frankly where her liberal-mindedness had gotten her. What if he *was* cheating on her? Should he be allowed to rest so easily?

A second passed, and she popped on the light. His head moved groggily, and she said, "Are you having an affair?"

"What?"

"Are you having an affair? I said."

His hand was already reaching for the light. "Forget it," he said, as she caught his hand, cutting him off at the pass. He wasn't getting off the hook so easily.

"I said, Are you having an affair?"

"And I said forget it."

"Forget it?" she said in disbelief. "We just said our marriage is going to hell, that's all. We've been married for a grand total of eight months—" She paused here for added drama, to let that sink in. But Boyle showed no emotion other than surprise, his eyes finally opening, his jaw ajar. He was listening.

"My God, it just dawned on me," she said. "We're not even gonna make a year. I always thought we'd make a year at least."

Well, if that was all that was bothering her . . . "For you, we'll make it," he said.

"For me?" That had to be the most ridiculous thing she had ever heard. "What about you? Offhand I'd say you got the better end of the deal—"

He was suddenly sitting up, and that meant she was scoring. "Oh, yeah?" he said.

"Yeah."

"You're saying I'm not a good provider?"

"That's not what I'm saying. You're a great provider—you provide a lot of laughs, a lot of grief. . . ."

She had to be doing something right because he was steamed. It was the most substantial conversation they had had in ages. "Yeah?" he kept repeating in that New Yorkish way he had been so swift to adopt. "Yeah? So what? Yeah? Just 'cause you get a check in the mail every week—you get money out of the mail like Jesse James. I work hard to lose that kind of money, whereas you—"

"Oh, you think it's magic? You think it just comes on its own with a little luck? Well, sure there's luck—"

"You admit there's luck?"

"Yeah, but you said the same thing about the stork. You're still trying to figure out where the hell babies come from. You think the whole world's some kind of conspiracy depriving you of your just due, favoring some and overlooking you. Well, I got news for you—to get ahead in this world, you gotta work for it."

"Oh, that's what you call it—getting ahead? Is that what you're doing?"

"To get a check in the mail, you gotta work for it."

But he was back to the other, insisting, "Yeah, but is that your idea of getting ahead? You call what you do 'getting ahead'?"

He was feeling sorry for himself and perversely hoped she would continue the attack so he could really wallow in the warmth of self-pity. She rose to the occasion, saying, "I call it working for a living."

That was a good start. They could build on that solid foundation and have a quarrel of real substance. "You think I don't work for a living?" he said, confident now they would soon be shouting at each other. He was feeling loose, getting in the old rhythm. It felt good. "You think I don't work? Whadda you think I do in Harlem all night?" He had raised his voice, and now predictably there was a banging on the wall from next door, urging them in no uncertain terms to knock it off.

She spoke softly. "I have no idea," she said, searching his face like a crack district attorney, peering into his eyes as far as the eye could see. "I've been wrestling with that horny issue every night. I have my suspicions."

"You think I don't work?" he repeated angrily, getting out of bed and reaching for his pants. Soon he was stuffing his feet in a single leg of the trousers, hobbling, off balance. She wondered where he was going at this hour of the night. "You oughtta see me sometime," he said. "You think I don't work—"

"How do you know I wouldn't like to?"

He ignored her. "When the people put money in the hat—the common paying Joe—*that's* when you're working. That's music! I wish you could see me sometime—"

"I'd like to," she said, adding, "if you'd ever invite me."

He seemed surprised that she would take him up on it. "Yeah? Well, get your clothes on," he said. "What time is it?"

"It's three o'clock."

She slipped out of bed and lumbered with her heavy figure toward the bathroom, reminding him of a heavily laden camel.

"That's all right," he said. "It ain't but midnight in Africa."

A minute later they came out of their apartment building, and he led her to a 1940 Buick, pushing her into the front seat.

"That's it. Get in," he said.

When she got in and tried the springy seat, she couldn't help recalling that only recently they had had no car. In fact, she couldn't remember their ever having a car. When he got in, she asked him, just out of curiosity.

"I didn't know we had a car," she said.

He put the key in the ignition and turned it. He certainly seemed to know what he was doing.

"Trombone player OD'd. I've had it since Thursday," he said, turning the key again. "Talk to me, baby."

"What would you like me to say?" she said.

He was talking to the car. The engine roared, and he mashed the gas, throwing her back in the seat. So this is the way he lives, she thought.

Chapter 9

HARLEM 1946, UPTOWN BY NIGHT. STRETCHES OF blue neon on hot pavement and ad hoc committee members calling roll under street lamps, no fear of being disturbed. A man is playing matador on his way to the suicide sofa, past junk shops, bars, instruments of torture. Home, dirty as it is. He stumbles with typical cravings, falls flat on the sidewalk, delighted with the result. It's a good moment to launch a new career.

The Buick pulls up in front of the Club 88. Johnny gets out of the car and comes around to open the door for Francine, music from inside the club filling the street, as he opens the back door, takes out his horn. Arm in arm, the two of them head inside, Johnny a little impatient with her and tossing aside a cigarette butt, only to see several darkies scuffle over it. He shoos them away, straightens his tie, and now he is ready.

"You wanted it, you got it," he said. "C'mon, I'll show you my secret life."

It's crazy inside, electrical before the electrical advent, bebop after supper, silk and somber. Someone is jumping amid a volley of oaths, powerful muscles under thin garments, a shout from the audience, and the band keeps playing. The quintet on the bandstand, Cecil Powell on trumpet.

Johnny finds her a seat, thanking a man who must be a gentleman to have given up his chair for her. He kneels beside her and listens. Those who know him salute, and his fingers are getting itchy. There's Cecil in the spotlight this very minute, turning to reveal his chunky silhouette.

"You OK? Sit tight," Johnny said to her, noting how big her eyes had become as a result of straining to see the faces behind the smiles in the dark. "These are nice cats. You'll be all right."

She looked at the high-toned couple sitting across from her, the two of them nodding drowsily from some potent combination. She thought they were nodding at her and nodded back with the slightest movement, just enough to encourage the foppish gent to offer her some of what he was having, Red Label in a glass. She shook her head. "No, I'm sorry," she said. "No, thank you, but I'm having a good time all the same."

She hoped the latter would assuage his feelings and wouldn't make him think that she had declined to drink out of his glass just because he happened to be a Negro. That was the last thing she wanted. His large

178

lips had nothing to do with it. Just then, Johnny reached out and set the glass back in front of her, changing her mind for her.

"Go on. Drink it," he said.

"But, Johnny, the baby—I—"

He insisted. "Drink it," he said again, sloshing the whiskey around in the glass. "I said drink it, goddamn it. It's our night out. I want you to enjoy yourself."

He might have added, "as much as I intend to enjoy myself," because in another moment he was gone, unable to resist the lure of the bandstand. He headed up the aisle, and they were playing his song. Amid shouts of approval and backslapping, he opened his case, and as her lips moved to the whiskey glass, he began to blow. Peering at him over the rim, she knew there were corners of his soul she had never known and never would. Only a pulmonary lesion could stop him now.

He was almost manic, hanging back from the melody, waiting for propitious moments to strike and then catching up and going ahead, blowing short bursts, sheets of sound that came across as tirades, lisping, tripping, sliding, swallowing, choking, rolling, a roaring success despite his double chin, something she had only noticed just now. He was getting a double chin, and what was she getting? A bellyful? A double belly? In the end, where did it get them—either of them? His terrible labor on the horn, her endless organization and reorganization of the apartment, closets and dresser drawers, antiroach food on every inch of the terrain. I mean, in the end what could you do but raise objections and struggle along? That's what most people did. But was it what she wanted? Black women had such provocative rumps. Maybe they were the specific cure for his melancholy, and that's why he came so often. She took another drink of the whiskey, was feeling shivery, and so she took another.

Johnny Boyle forged right ahead, playing with his

179

eyes closed, and therefore not seeing Francine put away one glass and then another, not seeing her either when she got up shakily to tango with the last of the red-hot hepcats, a black majordomo who did a double-take on seeing her puffed stomach but who led her off to dance anyway on the intimate floor of the bistro.

Johnny made his horn talk, pouring out his heart's woes ... woe number one thousand and one being when he awoke from his reverie and saw his wife dancing with another man, black hands on her white dress, her gaze turned toward him, half-drunk, looking over the hepcat's shoulder. He closed his eyes again, not willing to let even that haunting image intrude on his music, instead cutting loose with a wail on the sax. That about summed it up, but a minute later the music had ended and the problem hadn't. He saw Francine leave the dance floor with her newfound friend and head for the front door, and from all appearances the two of them were having a cozy go of it, Francine walking like a duck and evidently planning to go home with him. Her head was on his shoulder, and they were holding hands. Boyle saw red but didn't know what to do about it. For a minute he did nothing at all, fingering his saxophone, which was no use to him at all in such an emergency.

Angry at his own lack of decisiveness, which he was afraid would be misconstrued as fear, he might have stood there well into the next musical set, if Cecil Powell hadn't taken the initiative for him. Cecil had seen the same thing Johnny was seeing and reached out to take his saxophone, as one friend to another. "C'mon, man. Get going," he said. "I'll take care of that."

Johnny obliged without delay, handing over his horn and heading for the door. He only hoped it wasn't too late. He'd never forgive himself.

He came out of the club just in time to spot the colorful hepcat hopping into a taxi and shutting the door. Cloud cover was low and visibility was limited. The cab took off as Johnny gave chase and ran to the Buick, opening the door, jumping in, and fumbling with his keys. When the engine finally started, he cursed himself for taking so long and set about immediately making up the lost time, shoving the car into gear and leaving a streak of tire rubber behind. The taxi was now distant indeed, distant and taillights fading. He began to despair as he looked at the speedometer. The needle was rising but the oil pressure falling, and he knew it would take a miracle now. He had lost her, if he didn't watch out.

He wasn't a religious man, but he cried aloud for help. Fierce determination was the look on his face, teeth gritted. This was war. Any minute now they would be over Amsterdam Avenue, enemy air space, and the flak would begin, a layer of ack-ack so thick you could walk on it. He was thinking some of this, battening down the hatch, when a human hand reached over the back of the seat, followed by a moan, then a laugh, then a ridiculous giggle. The implications took a moment to sink in.

"Johnny," said the back seat.

His reflexes weren't the quickest. "Shut up," he said, telling whoever it was. Then he whirled and for a split second took his hands off the wheel. "Goddamn it! Francine!"

It was just long enough for him to lose control, and though he tried furiously to regain it, the car promptly hit a curb and rebounded back into the street, whereupon he gratefully slammed on the brakes just in time to be rear-ended by a slow Hudson. That was bad enough, but it wasn't nearly as tragic as it might have been. Boyle's earlier pleas to the Almighty hadn't gone ignored. The impact did little damage other than to knock Francine from the seat onto the floorboard, where she lay like a turtle, appendages pointing upward.

"I thought you were dead!" he said with emotion, ignoring the honking traffic that was forced to pass on either side of them, looking in the back as she slowly righted herself on her hands and knees, drunk and with a bad case of sniffles. She was wiping her nose with her finger, and Johnny passed her his handkerchief. "Where's your purse?" he said to her.

She rolled back onto the seat, babbling. "I don't know," she said. "I left it."

"Great. We'll have to go back."

"No, please—I don't wanna go back. I'm kinda embarrassed."

"Whadda you got—the whirlies?"

Dizzy, her hands moved to her eyes. "Yeah. The whirlies. I think I'll just pass out like a lady."

"Fine."

He was trying to get the car started again before the people from the Hudson could get out and fuck with him. He kept looking in the mirror, turning the goddamn key. He wasn't taking any chances. People in Harlem were crazy at five in the morning.

Meanwhile he wished Francine would shut up. She was starting to get on his nerves. "You want me to get drunk, Johnny—I'll get drunk," she said, as the motor caught in the nick of time. Two heavyset Negro women had gotten out of the Hudson and were approaching his window as he gunned the car and took off with a sigh of relief. "I sing better jazz when I'm drunk," Francine was saying. "If you want me to get drunk, that's what I'll do, Johnny—I'll stand on my head, attract a crowd, if that's what you want—I'll be more fun, fall down—I don't feel so hot."

"Just lay still," he said, scanning the horizon for possible new dangers. But there was only the sun coming up, beautiful even in Harlem. "I thought you were dead," he said.

"You thought I was dead?" She asked the question almost in tears, wondering how the idea could even occur to him. "I just wanted to see, Johnny. I never see you any more—and then those hairs on your shirt, that woman who keeps calling you—"

"What hairs on my shirt?"

"You know the ones—"

"I told you, it's pieces of flowers or something, flowers floating in the breeze—"

"Did you really do it with them, Johnny?"

"Whadda you want, the grand tour? New York? The sights? All the sights, I'll show you the sights—just hang on. I'll take you for a ride."

He turned the corner, wheels squealing. Fine. She wanted New York, he'd give her New York. If she didn't believe his quaint little story of flowers floating in the open air, he'd show her the squalid side. If corroborating evidence was what she was after, it could be arranged.

Thirty minutes later, the Buick moved past a block of gray apartment houses, and he pointed out the contours of the skyline.

"These are my old haunts," he said. "This is where Lenore lives."

She was crying. So it was true, she thought.

"Johnny, don't torture me—"

She didn't want any more, but the tour had just begun. There was much more to come. Same thing a little later, a different street, another port of call. Johnny pointed again, this time to an upper-floor apartment where a light was burning.

"I used to make the rounds. First Lenore, then Fifi. She's waiting up for me," he said matter-of-factly. "This is where Fifi lives."

"Fifi—" She couldn't believe what she was hear-

183

ing—a woman named Fifi in her husband's life. It hardly seemed possible, and then suddenly she had a new worry. She felt a stabbing sensation in her stomach and held her breath. The first pain was followed by another less than five seconds later. What else could it be? she thought, wiping the tears from her eyes, trying to shake her head clear of booze.

"Johnny," she said softly, praying it wasn't what she thought it was. But there it was again. She counted. Four seconds apart, and a strong urge to vomit. "Johnny—" she said, louder—"how fast will this car go?"

He didn't hear her. By now he was heading down a new street, examining the buildings on either side so as not to appear to choose at random, again pointing at a window like a million other windows.

How many windows in New York? The thought crossed his mind, and it occurred to him that no one in the world knew. "This is where Vivian lives," he said. "Her sister's across the hall. They've both had the various venereal diseases."

At the mention of venereal disease, she screamed, just as he had expected she would, though the violent nature of her reaction took him by surprise. She clutched her lower abdomen and expelled a mighty breath, and for the first time he felt perhaps he'd carried this little joke of his too far.

"Johnny! The baby!" She winced. "It's coming! Oh, God—it's coming. Help me! Something's happening!"

"What is it?"

"Something's happening!"

He didn't doubt it for a minute. From the tone of her voice, he knew it must be so, and he went absolutely into shock, utterly disintegrating, able to think of one thing only. He didn't know where he was.

"The baby? You're sure? But it's too early," he said like a dunce, desperately looking around for something

184

that was familiar, only to remember he'd never set foot here in his life. It served him right, he thought. Now let's see him make a quick getaway when it really counted for something, and he didn't know where the hell they were.

"Johnny!" The pleas were enough to break his heart, and these were only the beginners. Wait till a few more minutes when things got serious and the baby decided to poke his head out and see what all the excitement was about. His brain went dizzy, the panorama of forbidding strange buildings before him. It was clear now what he had to do, but life was often like that, wasn't it? A transparency that made no sense. "Oh, Johnny, help!" she yelled.

"Where the fuck am I?" he said. "Hospital—where's the—? What borough's this? Is this Queens? Am I in Queens?"

"I thought you knew the neighborhood," she groaned. "Johnny, please! Can't you ask Vivian?"

She was willing to take help from any source, but Boyle was no help at all. He was hysterical. "I don't know where the fuck she lives! How would I know? I never seen her before in my life. It's just nothing—I made her up—"

Baby or no baby, she hugged him, so glad. But Boyle was still talking to himself, counting on his fingers, going goo-goo in the family sedan.

"You made them all up?" she said. "Fifi—and—?"

"Yeah. All of 'em. You know I couldn't cheat on you, baby," he said, trying to remember the route they had taken to get here. "That hospital—I saw it—where was it? We just passed it—"

She didn't care. "Johnny, do something!" she said.

When in doubt, back up. He backed the car up to get the lay of the land, so to speak. They were both berserk.

Chapter 10

ANYWAY IT WAS A FALSE ALARM. THAT AFTERNOON Johnny sat in the car and listened to baseball, waiting for her to come out of the hospital. The close call had had an unsettling effect on him. It had made him face the future, and he discovered that it scared him, made him lament the passing of his youth, the precious few weeks of freedom remaining to him before the birth of his firstborn. It was the fifth inning before he knew who was playing, and the bottom of the ninth when she finally emerged, squinting into the sunlight.

When she climbed in the front seat, she noticed the change. Something was bothering him. She could always tell something was wrong when he gave her flowers, and these he handed her now were by far the nicest he'd ever bought, lots of different colors bound together by a gorgeous red bow.

"Stunning?" she said, showing off her round figure, needing reassurance that he didn't see her as ungainly as she herself felt. She gave him a peck on the cheek.

"For you," he said with a sick little smile.

She sniffed them and blushed. She still felt foolish for the night before, when she'd made such a big deal over so little, in retrospect, the false alarm and whatnot. Maybe that was what was eating him, but, then, how was she supposed to have known last night wasn't the real thing? She'd gone in with every good intention, holding her breath and exhaling as the nurses told her to. It just wasn't her time yet, and she wished he'd try to be mature and understand that fact. She wanted the baby every bit as badly as he did.

"Well, they sure sober you up in a place like this," she said finally. "They sure dry a girl out."

He nodded and started the car. "I know you like roses," he said, "but I liked the daisies, and the yellow was nice, but pink's your favorite . . ."

That's all he talked about for the first few blocks, the flowers, and she wondered why. She wondered what was really on his mind, but he obviously wasn't going to say, because after the first few blocks he didn't say anything at all. They just drove along, and he was thinking to himself that he'd been lucky this time. The kid had shied away at the last minute, but once he got it in his head to come down the chute, he'd come, and there'd be no stopping him. Boyle could almost hear the little squirt gloating. Francine was ready, the kid was ready, and the only one who wasn't ready was now trying to figure a way out of the dilemma. He knew Francine wouldn't be content to stay at home forever, and then what? The kid would move in with his father, and one of them would have to go to work. What kind of life for a kid was that? A kid belonged in school, not scrimping for a living in poverty and privation.

So it was inevitable that Boyle should today feel panicky on the way home from the hospital, wringing his hands, smoking cigarettes one after the other, until even the fresh flowers began to droop and seemed to gasp for air. By the time he reached their delightful little apartment, he wasn't saying a word, but he had already decided to leave his wife for his child's sake.

A few nights later, Francine opened her eyes in the darkness of the bedroom and found herself alone, as usual. Her first instinct was to look at the clock, wondering whether by some off chance he had come home yet, and tonight, at least, she ventured to say the miraculous had occurred. The sound of soft piano chords drifted in from the living room and greatly

187

picked up her spirits, as the song he played was theirs—"New York, New York"—and the mere fact that he had chosen it gave her grounds for optimism in the long night ahead. He might be in a romantic mood, she thought, and failing that, perhaps a civil one. It had been so long since they had even touched one another in a caring way that she was starved for him and had lately taken to grasping at long shots, no matter how remote.

She had swung her swollen ankles out of bed, switched on the lamp, and was halfway into the robe when she heard her slim hope fade. The music was terminated abruptly with a thud, indicating its player's displeasure as he hammered the keys and brought down the cover. When he came in a minute later, she was still half in her robe and half out of it, sitting on the edge of the bed, in a wretched mood.

He was loosening his shirt, and when he saw she was still up, came around the bed. He had a kiss for her, an onomatopoeic smooch right between the eyes.

"Hi, babe," he said. "You awake?"

If he had to ask silly questions, why did they have to be such stupid ones? She shook her head. "I just got up. What time did you get in?"

"I forgot to punch. Just now," he said. "You wanna itch my back?"

He hiked his shirt, revealing his bare back. This apparently was a regular ritual between the two of them, as was no doubt her reply. "Itch it yourself. I scratch mine," she said.

But she scratched anyway, as Johnny dropped his pants on the floor like a ten-year-old and stepped out of them without picking them up.

"Where's my pajamas?" he said.

"In your drawer."

He went to the drawer, got his pajamas and came back. She resumed scratching and asked him the natural question, since he was home unusually early tonight.

"Did you see Paul?" she said.

That supposedly had been his evening's destination. Paul had called yesterday to say he was in town and to give them the good news that the band had a New York gig—nothing like the old days, but then what was? She had said they'd come to see him, of course, but he wanted to lock it up tight. He and Boyle and some of the others could get together for good cheer, and if one thing led to another, Johnny might like to sit in. A good sax man was always worth a round of drinks, and if one thing led to another, he might like to come with the band when they moved on to Pittsburgh. Wasn't Boyle from Pitt originally? She had said yes and added that it was a great idea, just the sort of thing Johnny needed to get back some of his enthusiasm for rational music and rational people. Of course, Paul didn't want to take him away when she was in need of moral support ... but she said, on the contrary, it was Boyle who was most in need of it, and that in any event when the time came, Johnny could hop a train back and be with her by the time she came to in the recovery room. This was 1946, after all, and giant strides had been made. To all of that, Paul said, Fine, and then included some personal thoughts for her. She vowed to put Johnny in touch and thanked him ever so much for the call. She hadn't felt happier in recent memory. It wasn't often that a call accomplished so much.

Then it came time to implement the plan, and she had turned to Johnny. At first he had been cool to the idea, then positively frigid, then cool again, and finally she had prevailed upon him to have a drink with the guys at least. He might even find a white person he liked. You never could tell, and finally he shrugged and said sure, he'd go.

So now she was asking him, "Did you see Paul?"

"Paul who?" he said, getting there in roundabout fashion. "Paul Wilson? Sure, we got together, had a few drinks—I took him to a couple of hot spots, went out on the town—"

"That's funny." She frowned. "He called here about eleven and said you never showed up."

He turned to stare at her, that blank, puzzled expression he had to have been born with. "He called here?" he said.

"Yeah. He said he was still waiting in the hotel bar. Wasn't that where you agreed to meet?"

"What's this? A cross-examination?"

"Well, isn't that where you were supposed to meet?"

"Sure. The hotel bar, right? Why? He said I didn't meet him there?"

"That's what he said."

He pretended to be even more puzzled, slipping into his pajama top, while she continued to scratch him, scratching him on his stomach, increasingly digging in with her nails, whether she meant to or not.

"He said I didn't meet him at the hotel bar?" he said, still trying to be perfectly clear about this thing. "Is that it?"

"That's what he said."

"It doesn't make sense," he said, giving a performance worthy of an Oscar. "I mean, the nerve of the guy. Why would he lie about something like that? You take a guy out, you show him a good time, talking, drinking—and look how he acts in return. Makes you wanna renounce your citizenship, for chrissake—"

"You didn't go, did you?" she said, inadvertently catching him with a fingernail, causing him to recoil.

"Ow, goddamn it, Francine, you nicked my tit."

"I was going for the jugular," she said, smoothing over the affected area of flesh. "You didn't go over

190

there, did you?" He turned, looked at his chest in the mirror. "Why didn't you go?" she asked him.

"Something came up, that's all. I really wanted to go."

"You didn't wanna go. You're lying."

"You're right," he said. "I didn't wanna go. What for? I don't even wanna see the guy, much less play with him—the kind of shit he plays."

He guessed his tit was okay and tucked it back in his pajamas, buttoning up.

"So what're you gonna do?" she said.

"I'm gonna stay here and have the baby—any objections?"

He was still pouting in the mirror, impersonating a woman, and he didn't do it at all badly, combing his hair until it was just too exquisite.

"And then what?" she said.

"Nothing." His face looked at her in the glass, hardening like a dowager's. "Nothing. I'm gonna stay here and have the baby—I love my baby—if he gets outta line, I'll make him play jazz for a living. Any other questions?"

"Why bother?"

He thought the time propitious to say something he'd been intending to get off his chest for a long while. It was important enough for him to turn around and look her in the eye. "You know, Francine," he said philosophically, "you're gonna make it. I'm looking at you here, sitting on that bed, the bed I also sleep in—and it occurs to me you're going to make it. You're going to make it in this wonderful world of ours. Every night in bed I touch you, and yet I realize only half of us are going to make it. No matter how hard I hang onto you, nothing can change the fact that you're a singer with a wonderful talent—"

She didn't know what to say. She'd never quite seen him like this before, and she had seen him a lot of ways. A simple thank you might be in order. "Thank you," she said, "on behalf of my mother, my father . . ."

"And I'm not," he continued right through her thank you. "I'm just the other half of the bed. All my life it was the big bands, and when I get ready the first time, it's World War Two—very convenient for *them*—and when I get ready again, when I get out, it's all over, and the real war's just starting. The bands are through, and the funny thing is, I can't even stand their music any more, and this was my dream . . ." His voice trailed off, but then he came back to her, who at this point, he wished to emphasize, was the more important of the two. "So no matter what else I do," he said, "always remember I told you this: You're gonna be a star someday."

"Oh, please—"

"You will be."

He was being so nice and silly, she wanted to reach out to him and take his hand, but he walked away. He was leaving the room, and suddenly it occurred to her that he had been perfectly serious. All that stuff. He was trying to say goodbye, and it didn't make any sense.

Chapter 11

FINALLY, WHEN THEY PULLED UP IN FRONT OF THE modest off-Broadway supper club where Paul's band was appearing, the double bill read BERNICE THOMAS, with "The Paul Wilson Orchestra" trailing far behind. It wasn't much of a place, but even so . . . (I think the name of it was Harry's but I could be wrong. It doesn't exist any more.) It was just the principle of the thing. Boyle was bitter on several counts, of which I'll mention a couple. It was disgusting to him that such a singer could get a prime billing, no matter how lousy the band. The band couldn't be that lousy—no way. That was number one, just a sign of how the times were moving. Number two, despite what he'd said, he resented that it wasn't his band he was walking in to see. He felt odd going in as a spectator. And number three, he resented losing the argument to come here tonight in the first place.

Francine had talked him into it. She had to see the gang again, she said, all of them together, and on the latter score he accused her of dwelling in the past. It was a phrase he used often, as it was one of his own.

"Stop dwelling in the past," he had said to her on the way over, looking in his rearview mirror often enough to see Ellen Flanery and her date necking in the back seat. God, he thought, the girl has no morals. Her date was sticking his hand up her leg, and she didn't care who saw. He wondered if a dame like that could ever be truly happy. "Stop dwelling in the past, Francine," he told her, as she recounted one amusing experience after another.

"Remember the time in Lordsburg?" she would start to say.

And he would cut her off by saying, "No, I don't remember."

"That's right," she would correct herself. "That was before you were with us. That was with Paul."

He would sizzle and look in the mirror. Unbelievably, Ellen's date now had slid his hand under her blouse. Pretty soon and he'd be sucking her zooms. That would be a sight to see. If they could just keep at it a while longer . . . but now they were coming up to the club, and Johnny with a rise in his pants.

He (vaguely) heard Francine talking to him from the other side of the front seat.

193

"Johnny, I promised Paul we'd be here tonight," she said.

He even heard himself say, "Yeah, well, if what he plays sells, I don't wanna hear it."

"Because you're not selling it," she said.

"No? 'Cause I'm not buying it."

Now they were even having a fight, and his voice seemed disjointed from his body. He couldn't defend himself. He had a boner from watching Ellen and would have liked to watch her swing her legs around the guy, except that Francine pointed suddenly and said, "Johnny, we're here. Where're you going?"

He pulled the Buick over. Ellen sat up in the back seat in the most rigid manner, straightening her clothing and pushing the guy away. From the sigh he made, it sounded like he had pulled a muscle, and Johnny could sympathize. As everyone else got out of the car, he wondered why he had never fucked Ellen himself. Probably it was because he had too much class, but that had never stopped him before, and it didn't stop her from giving him an enormous erection now. He told the others, "I'm gonna go park the car."

Francine gave him a look and slammed the door. She wasn't in a good mood tonight, and he didn't know why—he was his usual charming self. He sped off, leaving them to go inside without him.

"I'll be right back" were his parting words, something ominous about them, like the man who went up to the corner grocery for a loaf of bread and never returned, and his wife who waited seven years before she called the police. There was something of that in both of them just now, the looks they exchanged.

Once inside, the headwaiter, maybe the only waiter in this less-than-regal joint, met them in the doorway, and Francine presented them, saying, "The Francine Evans party, please."

"You're with Mr. Boyle," said the waiter, recalling

194

the reservation, maybe the only reservation of the night.

"Don't rub it in," she said.

"This way, Mrs. Boyle."

It made her feel like a hundred to be called Mrs. Boyle, and up until recently it wouldn't have bothered her, but now it had such a stuffy sound to it as she followed the waiter forward.

On the bandstand, Paul Wilson had his back turned, leading the band. It was smaller than before, maybe only ten guys, all in white dinner jackets and playing champagne music, music you could eat to. Bernice did a wilted rendition of "Do Nothing Till You Hear From Me," and it seemed some things never changed. Paul turned in the middle of the song to wave hello. What the hell, it was like a high school assembly. He knew Ellen from a foxhole and Francine from forever, but he had to admit Francine had seen better days. Her cheeks were puffy, and from the size of her, it looked like Boyle had loaded her with a nine-pounder.

DISSOLVE TO another song by Bernice, "For All We Know" . . . and for all they knew Boyle wasn't going to show up tonight. People looked at their watches, Francine . . . Ellen . . . a lot of New York irregulars who wandered in off the street and wondered when the stripper would stop singing and start taking it off. Francine even got a couple of invitations to dance.

"No, thank you. I'm with someone," she told the creep at first. When he asked her again five minutes later, she pushed away from the table, pointing out her swollen condition. He pushed off.

"Where's he parking it anyway?" Ellen said. "Long Island?"

Francine looked at the time and signaled the waiter. She wasn't going to let it spoil her evening, because that's what he wanted. Nothing was going to get her

195

down tonight, she was determined, her first night out since the Harlem debacle.

"Well, where *is* he?" Ellen said, still wanting an answer.

"He likes to park cars," Francine said. "It's his favorite thing." Then she told the waiter, "I'll have another Seven-Up. Make that a double."

She was getting depressed in a hurry, but she should have counted her blessings. The real fun wouldn't start until several agonizing songs later, when Bernice would look up from the mike to see Johnny appear at the back of the room. Her heart would flutter and there he would be, standing in the doorway like Samson wearing a suit and a rumpled appearance. He was there representing the true music, and at any moment he would send the walls crashing down on the orgy lovers. In the tradition of the true music, he was also drunk. He had taken advantage of the hour or so he had been gone to get into the most obnoxious of moods, and when he confronted the headwaiter, he knew what he had to do. A vision flashed before his very eyes.

"Good evening. I've been parking the car," he said.

"Yes, sir?"

As the waiter looked on, Johnny ambled into the room, but not toward the table where Francine was sitting. Rather, like a bad dream from the past, he began to clap mockingly and walk toward the bandstand across the dance floor. His eyes were on Bernice, whose eyes were on him.

Francine was now watching him with the most pained expression anyone could imagine. It was the same thing Johnny had done at The Greenbrier when he came down from New York to be with her that first time . . . it was *hers*, the memory was treasured, and now Johnny was simply throwing it away, throwing it in her face for what it was, just a gag in his repertoire.

Ellen's date had had a most interesting evening. He

196

was an insurance broker who had never met a guy like Boyle in his actuarial tables, and when he saw tears in Francine's eyes, he understood even less of Boyle's sense of humor. At first he'd thought the guy was funny. Now he wasn't so sure.

"What's he doing?" he asked Ellen.

"He's drunk. Come on, let's dance."

Trying to save her best friend the embarrassment, Ellen practically dragged her date to the dance floor, but for Francine there wasn't any rescue. She looked on helplessly as Johnny walked all the way down front and took a seat. He was still clapping, and now he began to slap the table, cheering.

By the time Paul Wilson became aware of what was going on, he must have thought he'd seen this B picture before. Boyle was reaching in his wallet, handing the waiter a large tip, and in general making an ass of himself. Quite the man in control of things, the big spender so in control he had trouble getting the words out of his mouth.

"Beautiful, Bernice," he yelled up to her, slurring it. "That's perfect! You learned the keys, you learned the notes—that's good! Good sound! Good sound! You got it, Paul, that's it—let it swing. Swing it."

He leaned back in his chair, more pompous than ever, saw Francine alone at her table, and waved her over. He had to be out of his mind. She just looked at him, and he at her, grinning, as if to say, "How'm I doin'?" When she didn't smile, he shrugged, turning back to where the fun was.

"That's it, guys. That's it. Let is swing. Let it swing."

He was swinging from side to side exaggeratedly, out of synch with the band's sedate style, as the waiter approached with a bottle of champagne in a bucket . . . Johnny opening his wallet again, another tip, then waving the man away, wanting to do the honors himself.

But before that happened, the song mercifully ended, and Bernice spoke into the mike in her low, too-serious tone.

"We'll take a break now. Thank you for your attention."

Johnny, however, didn't believe in taking breaks, and he didn't. He kept carrying on as though the band was still playing. There was absolutely no difference in his behavior, and it was the greatest insult to the band he could think of. He was still swinging, and there wasn't any music. In other words, there wasn't any difference.

"That's it. Let it swing. Swing it! Swing it, you guys—hey, that's it. Now you're swinging—"

They were all staring at him, Paul Wilson, his old comrades-in-arms from the band—all just staring at him as he stopped and popped the cork. When it blew, champagne flowed over everything, and he finally got quiet, seeing the unamused looks on their faces. Champagne was running down his arm and over his only good suit, but he didn't care. What was a suit to a sport like him? Weren't they having a good time, like old times?

"C'mon, I'll buy you a drink," he offered all of them.

They gave him one look and walked the other way, all heading over to join Francine at her table . . . Johnny watching them go, watching them hug her one by one, their laughter, their horsing around, most of all their affection for one another . . . and he couldn't help wondering where he had missed the boat. He'd married her and tried to do all the right things, and despite that, tonight, as much as the first night they met, he was still on the outside and looking in at these characters. Not that it mattered to him, but what did it take to become one of these guys, anyway? It made him resentful.

He was almost enjoying feeling sorry for himself when a voice in his ear spoke up as he was crying in his champagne. "Hello, Johnny," it said.

He turned and saw Bernice. She still had a mad crush on him and appeared ready to throw away her career and follow him on the slightest provocation.

"If it ain't Bernice, the singing pigeon," he said. "How are you, Bernice?"

"You heard me. What do you think?"

She came a step closer, making him nervous.

"Aw, Bernice, you're just unbelievable," he said. "I never heard anyone sing like you, you know that? I never told this to anyone before, but you carry a tune like a hot turd."

"I know it," she said, in the mood for romance. "I'm quitting tonight. The only reason I came to New York was to see you."

"See me? I'm married, Bernice."

He took a step back, but she followed. His eyes were darting to Francine's table, where his wife and her buddies were all looking at him, drilling holes in him and Bernice. *If looks could kill* . . . Francine looked infuriated and ready to leave if either of them made another move, and Johnny himself realized the situation was getting out of hand. He suddenly wasn't sure if he had intended any of this to happen. He felt embarrassed, having no choice any more but to start dancing with Bernice in order to avoid her embrace. There wasn't any music, but plenty of heat, just the two of them dancing alone, and Johnny was reminded out of the blue of a *National Geographic* picture he had once clipped, the Bali dance of fire. Bernice put her head on his shoulder, and he looked over at Francine. She was troubled, to say the least, beginning to understand how difficult life must have been for him on the road.

"I'm married, Bernice," he said once more.

"But you don't love her."

"Sure, I love her."

"No, you don't. You love me." She spoke with such certainty that it mystified him. Her brain had to be confused, even doing the foxtrot. The shuffle of their shoes on the floor was the only sound in the club, the occasional *clomp* of her heels, the swish of her petticoats.

"I don't love you, Bernice. I can't even stand you," he said, but she wasn't listening. Either that or she knew it was his infamous sense of humor. How could he make her listen?

"You know how I know you love me?" she said.

"How?"

" 'Cause you always told me you hated my singing. That's when I knew that it must be something else."

She gave him a kiss on the cheek, and Johnny was even more amazed that he found himself where he was, doing what he was doing . . . dancing at close quarters with a singer while his pregnant wife looked on.

The week before, exceedingly horny one night, he had visited a prostitute. "My wife's in her eighth month of gestation," he had said.

He handed the young black girl a ten, and she said, "I understand."

He wished all human relationships could be that simple and honest, but here was Bernice with her eyes closed, for chrissake, her lips like hot coals burrowing into his neck. God knows she was dreaming of a hearth someplace in the Rockies, Winter Carnival and Paris in Springtime all rolled into one. Then he felt a tap on his shoulder.

"May I cut in?"

At last, he thought. With a sigh of relief, Johnny let go and turned, just in time to have the breath knocked out of him. It was a Paul Wilson punch straight to the solar plexus, followed by one to the face, landing square on that wondrous handsome mouth of his that made the good sounds. He went down in a heap on the dance floor, and Bernice immediately flew to his aid.

"Johnny——"

He was on his hands and knees, dripping tiny portions of blood on the polished teakwood, nothing more than a scratch really, searching for a handkerchief and muttering in disbelief, "He got me on the lip—he busted my lip!"

"Get up, Boyle." Paul was straddling him like a gunfighter, daring him to get up for the second round in the dusty street of Cimarron. "Get outta here, or I'll give you another one! C'mon, get up!"

"C'mere, Johnny," Bernice said and tried to cuddle him, when all he really wanted was to get up and make a grab for Paul. But Paul was already standing safely behind a wall of reinforcements from the band, and it was they who pulled Johnny to his feet and pushed him toward the exit, joined by a burly bouncer or two, and just when it seemed he didn't have a friend in the world, he called on the one person he knew he could always count on when the going got tough.

"Francine! Francine!"

He shouted it several times (as if the name itself held power) but kept being propelled toward the door, hands appearing seemingly out of nowhere to assist him on his way. Only Bernice stuck by him through it all, unwilling to let go until the very end.

"Get her the hell away from me! Goddamn it, Bernice!" he said, taking a swing at her and knocking her to the floor, where she was nearly trampled by the herd. But he didn't look back; he kept bitching, incensed that his shirt had also been ripped. "Take your hands off of me—I'll go! Francine!"

But he didn't see her, and was shoved out of the club and onto the sidewalk, where he recovered his balance and got his clothes back in order, still feeling sufficiently unrepentant to yell at the front door, now closed to him, "Francine!"

Unrepentant and persecuted, too, as he shook his fist at the vast, encircling conspiracy. "Gimme my wife!" he demanded absurdly, as if someone had taken her from him in the first place.

When nothing happened, he walked on up the sidewalk, looking much as he had the night of V-J Day so long ago, but now the street was deserted and he was alone. Maybe it was better this way, he thought, looking at the dark buildings on either side. It was as it should be. No parades, no confetti for him, please. He didn't want anyone to make a fuss. He had done what the situation called for and nothing more. One of them would have had to do it sooner or later, and it was better if he did it now. He had merely done his duty, and he didn't doubt that any other loving husband would have done the same.

The sidewalk rumbled from the IRT beneath, and he felt a vibration course through him from head to foot, a rhythmic jolt he thoroughly enjoyed. New York.

Chapter 12

AT THE CLUB 88 THE NEXT NIGHT, FRANCINE SAT FOR a moment in the back of the taxicab, making up her mind about going inside, screwing up her courage.

Inside, the jukebox was playing, and the nighttime regulars were on their marks ... subterranean types who preferred the darkness and the heavy air of low-lying places ... Johnny Boyle among these, sitting at the bar, flanked by Cecil Powell and a couple of laughing ladies the color of *café con leche*.

Cecil saw her first and gave Johnny a nudge. Johnny turned. "I see her," he said.

Her voice came faintly from clear across the room, her rotund figure standing in the doorway, framed by lamplight.

"Johnny—" she said.

He got up, and the laughing ladies beside him were suddenly stilled, whispering to themselves as he walked slowly across the room and stood before her for a second or two without speaking, at least without using words. Their eyes remained on one another and said more than either cared to verbalize. Then Johnny said, in a burst of originality, "So what's up?"

The laughing ladies laughed, and she slapped him hard, the hardest she had ever struck anyone in her life. She was surprised herself at the force of the blow, but Johnny didn't react. He just stood there, while she ran a hand silently over the red spot on his cheek, as if attending his pain, her pain as well, as it always would be . . . now straightening the part in his hair with her fingers. . . . He shrugged her off, avoiding her touch, evidently self-conscious in view of the others watching.

She understood. "That's what's up," she said.

"What?"

"A year of my life," she said, reaching into her purse. "It's all up. So are you. You know what this is?"

He looked down, and for an instant knew panic, feeling something pressed against his stomach that sure looked like the real thing. It certainly looked like a pistol she was holding, and before he could utter a word, her lips were on his. "It's the kiss of death," she said.

He was filled then with the meaning of terror, but also the sense of inner peace that comes when one gives oneself up to the inevitable and accepts that death is at hand. "So plug me," he said.

Instead of plugging him, she turned the gun so that he could see it was in reality only a plastic replica with a rubber-tipped projectile protruding from the barrel, and then, without making a big to-do about it, she simply crammed the muzzle down the front of his pants and pulled the trigger. *Bong!* There was the sound of a coiled spring mechanism firing the projectile, and she said as she walked away, "Keep it. You'll need it where you're living."

There was a gasp from the laughing ladies, who had never seen anything like it in all their years but had to admit the young woman had soul. She had left him doubled over with the toy gun stuck in his crotch.

Chapter 13

THE LONG-ANTICIPATED BLESSED EVENT FINALLY came two weeks later; picture, if you can, Paul Wilson and Tony Harwell at a couple of public phones, side by side in a hospital corridor, going through Francine's matchbook collection in an effort to locate the expectant father.

It was a distasteful task the two men were embarked upon, men who thought little of Boyle in private, but since it was important to Francine, they had agreed to do their best, even if it seemed the odds were against them. Boyle hadn't been home in a week, and there were at least sixty matchbooks in the glass decanter, all advertisements for bars and nightspots clear on the other side of town. But they had to begin somewhere, and Paul dropped a nickel in the slot and took his first handful.

MATCHBOOK MONTAGE, fingers dialing, placing calls ... producing results, as an hour later Johnny Boyle comes to the phone in Harlem. He's still carrying his saxophone, bedlam and music in the background. Paul lets him have it, saying, "She's having your kid. You coming or what? Just tell me so I can give her the word—"

Any other night Boyle might have come, but tonight was a different story. "No, I can't make it tonight," he said. "I'm playing with Monk. Tell her I'll be there first thing in the morning."

Paul himself was mildly impressed to hear that Boyle was playing with the much admired Thelonious Monk and couldn't resist asking, "Yeah? You're playing with Monk, no joke? What kind of guy is he?"

They talked music for a minute, and then Paul was forced to break off, remembering the reason for his call. Besides, Johnny was wanted back at the bandstand.

"Sure, pal, don't interrupt your set," Paul said. "If it was you instead of her, she'd be the first one here."

He could hear Thelonious Monk in the background, and he hung up. Monk was terrific, no question about it.

The next morning, Johnny came quietly into Francine's private room. A nurse moved the curtain to give him access, and he saw Francine lying there pale on the bed, her eyes closing on hearing him approach.

"I know those footsteps," she said.

"Mr. Boyle, when you're finished—"

He turned to look at the nurse and nodded, waiting for her to leave the room. When the door clicked shut, the silence was extraordinary, and he ran his fingers over his hat, turning it over in his hands. He had a jumbled collection of odds and ends he wanted to say but had nothing prepared. He felt a tremendous solitude but vowed to say only sunny things, seeing the sun come through the window.

"Trains ran late. I guess I missed the picture," he said.

"Paul told me," she said. "Congratulations."

"For what?"

"For playing with Thelonious Monk. Congratulations."

"Same to you. Sorry I missed it."

"I didn't really expect you," she said. "It's just one of those silly things the world expects, like going to funerals, and since neither of us are the type, I didn't really expect you. I wouldn't have come myself, except my presence was indispensable."

"Yeah, somebody's gotta be here," he supposed.

They were quiet, and he was about to ask if she'd written any poetry, when she said, "Oh, it's pretty pointless anyway. They knock you out. I could have been on Mars for all I knew." She looked at him, and he looked tired, like he'd lost weight. "Been eating away from home a lot, haven't you?" He didn't say anything, and she patted a spot on the mattress. "Take a load off your feet," she said, having a hard time keeping back the waterworks. "Share my bed."

He sat down and took her hand. Was that his palm sweating or hers? For the record, let's say it was both. Her nose was stopped up, and he wondered how long she'd been out from under. "The boxing kangaroo," she said, squeezing his hand tightly. "Ten rounds, the main event. He hits below the belt—they had to cut me, Johnny."

He'd been told. "If there's anything you want," he said. "If there's anything I can do—"

It sounded so woefully inadequate. What could he do, run an errand for her? Bring her magazines? The world wasn't fair, that's all. It was her operation and his visitation, and when you reached this point in the movie, it was expected that you come forward with a better offer than that—a reconciliation or something. But he had none, and she didn't expect any.

"Did you see him?" she said.

He'd looked in the observation window already, had pressed his nose to the glass along with the rest of the puzzled new fathers. "He's certainly a feather in your cap," someone said of his son. *His* son?

"Yeah, he's a little Republican, ain't he?" He smiled, remembering the pink little fists his son had made and waved menacingly in his direction.

"His name's Johnny, unless you object."

He felt like gushing tears himself and changed the subject, reached into his pocket and pulled out an item he had clipped from this morning's paper.

"Did you see Jo Stafford's review?" he said.

"Is she in town?"

"Here's the part that makes me crack up," he said. " 'Her road band proved itself an admirable swinging combo—' "

"What's wrong with that?" she said.

"You ever heard such nonsense? A singer's road band. 'Admirable swinging combo—' They wouldn't know one if they heard it. I could get a bunch of cigar-store Indians and put 'em behind Jo Stafford, and they'd get good reviews. Just goes to show, there ain't no bands any more—just singers and 'combos.' "

She didn't like his tone of voice when it came to singers but didn't feel like arguing with him under the circumstances. That was all behind them now, and instead she said, "I see your point."

He went on, citing the same source. "And get this, talking about Arnie Trench—remember him, your friend from Dorsey? He's with her now. '. . . her musical arranger, formerly of Tommy Dorsey note—' You hear that? That guy couldn't arrange his own funeral. He'd never been a band arranger, but he's arranging for her. It doesn't make sense."

"Maybe she got him the job," she said.

"Why would she do that?"

"Maybe she likes him."

The parallels to his own career were obvious, but Boyle had a short memory. He gave her hypothesis a shrug and chose to call upon the review for a final quote. "Calls him also 'an innovative soloist'—where have I heard that before?"

"It's what they said about Yehudi Menuhin," she said.

Then a strange thing happened. For a remarkable moment he forgot everything, everything that had gone between them. He forgot where he was and was fresh as a daisy, unaffected and smiling, as if the past didn't exist, or anything outside his own boyish ebullience. His gestures were animated, and listening to him talk was more than she could comfortably bear. It was precisely that part of him, the child in him, that she loved.

"There's a place in a Three Stooges movie," he said, and she had no idea what he was getting at. "I forget which one—where Moe is being chased by somebody and he's going out the window, see? It's a skyscraper or something, and as he's going out the window, these gorillas on his heels, he stumbles on this big steamer trunk, opens it up, and there's this fellow inside all tied up in ropes. And so Moe looks at this guy all trussed up and says—you know what the punch line is?"

Oh, God, why me? she thought. She was shaking her head, her cheeks streaming. "No. What's the punch line?"

"He opens the trunk, looks at the guy and says, 'I've found Yehudi!' Then he shuts the trunk and jumps out the window." She sniffed, looking at him blankly, as if something else surely followed. But there wasn't anything else. It was just his way of making an interesting observation, dredging up from nowhere a vignette that had nothing to do with anything. He explained.

"You said Yehudi Menuhin. It made me think of that," he said.

The words were just out of her mouth when she began to sob aloud. It was because she loved him still that she threw her head to the other side of the pillow and refused to look at him, biting the words. "Oh, God, if I never tell you again, I love you forever," she said, ostensibly giving him the cold shoulder. "Now get out of my life."

She had come to the realization that these should be her last words on the subject and chose to say nothing more. He quietly turned on his heels and went out the door. He had left behind his hat, but she didn't tell the nurse, thinking she wouldn't be able to stand the ordeal of seeing him again. One goodbye forever was enough for one day. If the hat was that important to him, he could always return for it, but she knew he wouldn't.

Anyway, the nurse drew the gauze curtain back in place and happened to remark, "You know, it's none of my business, but your husband has the most unusual smile."

Francine took the compliment with an unusual smile herself, her eyes glistening with tears. Now that it was over, she felt like she'd just taken a bad tumble and was lucky to have come out of the bone-shaker in one piece.

"Who gives a tumble?" she said.

The nurse appeared not to hear and went about her chores, a shadow through the gauze—a common theatrical prop. Francine closed her eyes, and a dream went floating down the river. CLOSE ON GAUZE, DISSOLVE TO:

Of course what followed was a movie all in itself, a marvelous Busby Berkeley musical, a Hollywood success story of the sort they don't make any more. Most of you know the rough outline: Girl rebounds from disastrous marriage, determined to get to the top. She makes it, but that's just shorthand. There's more to it than that. Life's no pushover for anyone, and she keeps struggling. Never call a person happy until she's dead, to paraphrase the old saw. Until then she's merely fortunate.

In 1947, a TITLE APPEARS on her screen: ONE YEAR LATER. APPLAUSE as she is introduced at Barb Kelly's Hat and Cane Club, and she steps to the mike, feeling her way. It's been a while since she's appeared in public, but she needn't worry. She's got her boosters. There's her agent, Tony Harwell, in the front row, and behind her on the bandstand, Paul Wilson leading her musicians, her combo. Not quite the old days, but this is 1947, and what do you expect, a big band? The sextet strikes up.

When she opens her hands midway through the first verse, we know there's something else she's got going for her, too—something she never had before. Call it something borrowed, something blue, it's Boyle's farewell gift, and it's the least he could do. If she has the pantomime and the gestures all right now, they're things she learned in the dumb show with him, a trunk of troubles she's now free to unload on the rest of us, and, my, how she does!

From the instant she began to sing, the audience was riveted to her. Here was more than just another voice, even another great voice. This was bruise time talking, souvenirs of the soul. A woman of legend with a rendezvous. By the time she introduced a song she had penned the words to, the joint was full of whispers. Where had she come from? Who was she?

"... a song written by a bebop musician one night, who didn't know what it was until I told him," she said. "Something by my first husband. 'New York, New York.'"

Her first husband indeed. The way she said it made it sound like she knew there would be others, maybe a long line of them. Artie Shaw could do it—why couldn't she? When "New York" concluded, they were

210

on their feet and yelling for more, even the sophisticates among them tied in knots of ecstasy. No need to wander ceaselessly, they shouted. You'll always have a home here. And they adopted her at once.

"Thank you," she said, flushed, coming back for an encore and further ovations. "Thank you so much."

1948 brought a sea of changing faces, different crowds. "New York, New York" was released on the Decca label, and people shuffled through a thousand record bins across America to make the song a hit ... hands paying money, cash registers ringing, her picture staring from the sheet music in music-store windows ... "New York, New York," as sung by Francine Evans. On every Main Street in America. It was her year, and there was nowhere still to go but up.

1949, a glossy autographed publicity still ... 1950, nightclubs across the country ... 1951, 1952, five-star reviews in *Metronome* and *Down Beat* ... 1953, her picture in *Variety* and the fan magazines, her son Johnny now six, going on seven. But whatever became of her husband? No, not her current fling with the romantic Neapolitan she had eloped with while on vacation in Italy, but her first one, whatzisname, the kid's father? Hadn't he been a musician at one time or another? What ever happened to him?

Well in 1947, Johnny was doing studio session work in New York, the only white guy in a colored group playing race music, but, as usual, working his style into groups wasn't his forte; and one day when he couldn't resist letting loose with a solo binge and screaming a little, the white producer in the control room flipped on the switch.

"Tone down that sax," he bellowed. "I'm hearing bebop instead of race music."

"What're you talking about?" Johnny said, begging to differ. "Where do you think bebop comes from?

Jazz is the black man's music, the American Negro gave the world jazz—"

"And the Italians gave it indigestion. Get out." The man jerked his thumb, meaning *Out*. "You want my job? Well, you can't have it," he said.

"Yeah? We'll see about that," Johnny said, slamming down the lid of his saxophone case and walking out. "We'll just see about that." But when he got to the door, he turned and said, "What the hell is your job anyway? Tell me, I wanna know."

"I'm an A and R man, you dumb fuck."

"Fine. I'll remember that."

But in 1948 he was playing raunchy sax in a raunchier dive, and 1949 found him doing the same. Ditto 1950, still blowing like a klaxon, squalling and squawking and blurred by the smoke, seeming not to realize that no one was listening. What good was being a lighthouse if the only people traveling by sea were other lighthouses? Meaning what? Simply that most nights his whole audience consisted of other jazz cats, and when he went to hear someone else, it was the same. Jazz was ahead of the public, and the gap was widening. One day even Boyle sat down to ask himself some hard questions.

Music had caused him to avoid the facts of life all his life, and the facts were these: He could play jazz, drink rotgut and fill his pipe for only so long. Already he was growing languid, and after a while only his eyes would be dreamy. The muse that gnawed at him would finally go and he would lapse into passivity. Then it would be over, with nothing left but the rotgut. The muse entrusted herself only to the young, and some days he was feeling old and gloomy. If only he'd gotten in on the ground floor, he reminisced. Goddamn the war. When he measured the rhythm of his life, he was certain he'd live only long enough to be penniless.

The world was a barren wasteland, and the artist the

bearer of water. But when the artist himself wasn't able to drink, he thought, who raised a cry? No one, he thought, driving himself mad thinking of the well-dressed men he passed every day downtown or sat next to on the subway. They looked like bullfrogs, their Adam's apples bulging over their tight neckties, uttering occasional croaks as the stickiness seeped out of them. He didn't want that—but what did he want? He didn't envy men who had lost their smile—but how to keep it? He analyzed his talents. Besides music, he had only the gift of gab, but surely in tandem the two of them amounted to something of value, a unique combination, if he could only figure out in what direction to point himself.

It was at about this time that the notion of being an A & R man gained appeal. The idea of having some jurisdiction all his own struck him suddenly on his thirty-second birthday as a desirable goal in life, and he decided to investigate the possibilities. A determining factor, too, was the sheer geography of the control room, looking down on the others, looming large above them for purposes of manipulation. This, too, played a careful part in his decision, as it agreed with his delicate psyche.

So though he continued to play sax and always would, he began to develop outside business interests as well, parlaying his royalty money from "New York, New York" into an office on Publishers' Row, where he began meeting the melody makers and prime movers. He learned that the business, any business, wasn't so complicated, once you learned the nuts and bolts of it, and in the early fifties there was excellent opportunity to take advantage of the existing confusion and slip in, posing as a virtuoso. No one knew what came next. The bands weren't around, singers made the public fickle. Country music was foreign, and race music obscene. Jazz? Forget it. But there was something else

213

coming along, something no one gave much credence to at first. Elvis stepped into a studio in Memphis, and there were some in New York who listened.

In 1955 Johnny made a record with the Five Satins called "Wonderful Girl." In the middle of the session there was a power failure. A fuse blew, or something, and while the engineer scurried to fix it, Boyle sat in the control room, calmly eating croissants and drinking coffee, at peace with himself, at one with the universe, and secure in the conviction that he knew a hit when he heard one. It seemed the *doo-daddy-wah* sounds agreed with him, and well they should, because in those days Rock and Roll was almost a shameful caper, a million dollars in sales for a few hours' work. Three or four artists on a given afternoon, no dress rehearsals, no wasted takes, no nothing—just certified gold everywhere the ex-jazz player turned.

To tell the truth, in a way it made him cringe whenever he thought of it, all the talented musicians standing in the unemployment line who couldn't make a go of it, and then to see some teen-aged creepo walk in one fine day and become idolized flesh before the month was out. There just wasn't any justice. But that was something Boyle had known for some time, armed from birth with the knowledge that the world was stacked against suckers, and by suckers he meant human beings, anyone who gave a damn about anyone else. So when it came time to take the money, he took it and gladly. Maybe it wasn't jazz, but let the human beings be the suckers. They bought it. He just produced it.

As for the music itself, it was so simpleminded it made him nauseated to listen to a B side after an A side, or even two A sides in a row . . . the same chord progressions over and over, record after record, G, E minor, C, D, or for a dramatic change of pace, C, A minor, F, G . . . *doo-doo-whop, doo-daddy-wop, duh*

214

doo-doo-wop, doo-daddy-wah. So primitive it didn't give the listener credit for any sophistication, it kept pounding the beat into you relentlessly. But, of course, Boyle realized only too clearly what had been his trouble before, his biggest mistake. In playing jazz, he had overestimated the intelligence of the American public. The American public had no sophistication, had no heart, or manners, either. It lived in an alcoholic vapor, watching propaganda films like a spasm of jelly on a movie seat, needing a blast of music every now and then only to light its light bulbs.

At home in his living room, Boyle preferred the spontaneity of jazz, the improvised fantasy of the moderns, Coltrane and Coleman. With jazz it was always possible to be surprised, whereas with rock and roll . . . anyway, what did it matter? Cold calculation told him you could get mighty rich playing to the tastes of the American public, and he had nothing but contempt for them, as he lit a Cuban cigar.

The control room was filling with smoke, and the engineer still hadn't located the source of the electrical trouble when Epstein, a bright and personable young lawyer, stuck his head in the door and said, "Johnny, the Sucrettes are here."

"Who?"

"The Sucrettes—the colored girls you heard at the Apollo."

"Right." Boyle remembered now and got up. He asked the engineer a question to which he already knew the answer and said he'd be about thirty minutes. Then he and Epstein headed up the hall, not talking about the Sucrettes but about swindles, not about music but about lies and legal complications.

The Sucrettes had shown admirable team spirit in their professional debut at the Apollo. Boyle had been there and had sensed big potential at once, not to mention a bigness in his crotch for the lead singer and her

215

rhythmic steps. By now a gourmet lover of Negro women, he couldn't live without them, liked them on the tall side, their long black legs preferably around his neck, their woolly triangles giving up their pink shrimp.

Now they were sitting across from him in his office with their garrulous Negro agent, a minister from the A.M.E. church who spoke a righteous blend of salvation and street jive. Boyle kept looking at the lead singer. He couldn't take his eyes off her, and he was afraid the agent would detect his interest and play his cards accordingly. But, Christ, she was extravagantly beautiful. Finally, he took a cold look at the situation and flipped on the RCA TV set behind him. It seemed rude, but the clergyman marked it up to the bohemian nature of the business.

"How long you been together?" Johnny asked them.

The agent responded, " 'Bout four months."

"You bring a demo?"

The man pushed a demonstration record across the desk, and Johnny picked it up, studied the title, turned in his swivel chair and placed the disc on a turntable. A little more confusion certainly wouldn't make any difference. Besides the sounds from the TV and now the record player, some enterprising lyricist was pounding the piano next door in search of the ever-elusive smash ditty, and Boyle found it difficult to concentrate. To make matters worse, the girls' agent insisted on telling him more about the formative years of the Sucrettes than he really cared to know, how they had come up the hard way, etcetera. Well, hell, hadn't they all? Boyle hadn't exactly grown up on the eighteenth tee of a country club himself, and the last thing he cared to hear now was how the trio had started together in the A.M.E. church, singing on Sundays, and that's where the good reverend had heard them the first time . . . blah, blah, blah . . . like diamonds in the rough . . . and had vowed to represent them then and there in any fu-

216

ture negotiations, strictly for charitable purposes, naturally. Like hell, Boyle thought. Old greedy black men could scramble for a dollar better than most, and he didn't like even the pretense of honesty. Honesty? Not in this world, preacher. Maybe the next, but don't bet on it.

He took off the demo and started to hand it back when his attention was suddenly riveted to the television screen at the mention of a familiar name. Whatever it was, it evidently took precedence over everything else. Without taking his eyes off the screen, he handed the record back to the preacher and said goodbye.

"Nice meeting you," he said without so much as getting to his feet. "All they need's a little polish."

"A little polish?" exploded the preacher, rightfully feeling insulted. "I thought we had an appointment. C'mon, girls, let's get outta here! These people crazy!"

The disappointed Sucrettes left their chairs to follow him, and Johnny looked up only long enough to follow the lead singer's retreating buttocks as she left the room. He then reached over and turned the volume of the TV up and called to Epstein over the intercom.

"Epstein, don't let 'em get away. Get 'em under contract before they leave the building."

His voice was perfectly matter-of-fact. It was, after all, a common negotiating tactic. The Sucrettes would be so thrilled he had changed his mind that they would settle happily for next to nothing. He smiled, settled back in his chair and watched the newscaster on the tube.

"Ending an eight-year absence from New York, Francine Evans arrived at La Guardia this afternoon," the newscaster read, and then she appeared amid a crowd of reporters at the airport, flashbulbs popping,

217

cameras raised overhead, the working press jostling for position.

"Miss Evans, how long will you be in New York?" they shouted. "What are your plans?"

She looked good. Boyle couldn't get over how good she looked. In nine years she had barely aged at all compared to him, but then, no doubt she had a Hollywood scalpel to thank for that. Everyone in Hollywood lived by the scalpel, he knew, but what the hell—she still looked like the girl in the WAC uniform he had met that night in an earlier lifetime, her irrepressible smile . . . and could her answer be mere coincidence?

"I'm doing a week at the Moonlit Terrace," she said into the battery of microphones in front of her. "I hope to be staying at least that long."

Who was that with her, there in the background? The one in the dark suit—was that Paul Wilson? Sonofabitch. And now making his way forward, Tony Harwell. The Three Musketeers, and Boyle's mind went blank. He hadn't seen any of the Musketeers since the war. He hadn't a friend to speak of.

"Any truth to the rumors?" they asked her.

"They're all true," she said mischievously.

That's my girl, he thought. Same old Francine. What a sense of humor. "The roses," he said aloud, talking to the set. "Look at the roses."

She was carrying a beautiful bouquet of red roses but seemed not to be conscious of them. A woman in her shoes, after all, was so accustomed to having flowers thrust at her that another batch couldn't be expected to make much of an impression, one way or another. How absentminded he had been to think of flowers when something more original was called for.

"You mean you and your latest leading man are more than just friends, Miss Evans?"

"Only on the screen. If I told you the truth, it would shock you," she said.

218

Cut back to the WNBC newsroom, and the newscaster is still chuckling over that one. "Now for the international news," he said, putting on a straight face.

Boyle clicked off the set and looked out his window, at the New York skyline, reminiscing about debauchery, old liaisons, but most of all about Francine Evans. She would always occupy a disproportionate share of his thoughts . . . the kind of laughter they had known . . . like he had said to her in the Notre Dame Café that time, the time when she watched him spill catsup all over himself. He had been talking about the supposed letters he had sent her after she had left him high and dry in New York that first time, and what was it she had said? He tried to remember. "What letters?" she had said. "You didn't send any letters—you didn't write. Don't tell me you wrote."

"See—you know, too," he had said to her for calling his bluff and setting him straight. Talk about having his number! She had known him so well, backward, forward, inside out. Now he could only smile and lament that things couldn't have been different in the end—but that was life. They had to pay their own way, and to each his own. All he knew for certain was that he would never meet anyone like her again, and for that he felt a certain relief. Relationships were for him impenetrably complicated, and in the midst of them, he always felt de-nutted to learn that his women weren't on his side at all, but were human beings just like the rest.

A couple of nights later, Francine opened at the Moonlit Terrace and was, as they say in the trade, Wow and Socko. She sang all the favorites and got many ovations. Boyle didn't make the performance, hung up in traffic as usual, but he did go up to her suite afterward.

There were the usual people and the usual flowers

219

on the usual white Steinway, and the usual best wishes. A black boy stood at the portable bar and wiped things with his rag. Francine couldn't be in two places at once, so many of the guests looked bored and milled restlessly like cattle in a chute, unable to think of anything in common with one another except a desire to see the star of the show and shake her hand. They had come here by many different routes—friends, relatives, relatives of friends, friends of relatives, the pigheaded rich who always invited themselves, the usual celebrities. Boyle was her only ex-husband on hand, but no one noticed. He saw Paul Wilson in the corner, but Paul didn't see him, and it was just as well. Paul was still leading a big band, for crying out loud, conducting the Francine Evans Orchestra wherever she went. What would they talk about—Benny Goodman?

Mostly he just stood alone, sipping his drink, not knowing any of these people, glancing across the room at her. She looked tired, he thought, but that was normal. She never failed to knock herself out at whatever she did, whether it was having a baby, putting on a show, or scrubbing walls. She was sitting on the sofa and exchanging matters theatrical with various pretenders she had never seen before, and probably she wished they would all go home and let her get some sleep. Aha, but with whom? That was the question. Boyle scanned the room and saw several possible candidates, lone wolves lurking on the periphery, waiting for the campfires to die down before they pounced. He wondered which one it would be, which of them would wangle a ticket to her bedroom before the night was over; but trying to guess her taste in men proved beyond him. To tell the truth, he couldn't see much in any of them that might attract her, and he was sure she would back him up in this. They were all prissy types, stage-door Johnnies and Ivy Leagers drinking complicated drinks, hardly a man among them.

220

He looked back at her. She was still locked in conversation, bored, nodding her head. Well-wishers could be merciless, and probably it was nothing more than her own fatigue that caused her to seem so blasé when their eyes finally met. At the bottom of it all, her heart still beat faster; the drawbridge still came down. She didn't get up at once, but excused herself little by little, coming over to shake hands with the man she still loved, getting kissed and hugged by strangers along the way.

"Love"? Yes, oddly, she still loved him. She regarded him as sloppy work, but that didn't mean she didn't love him. She had no regrets for anything she'd ever done and wasn't about to start by citing this or that foul blow. He had committed no act of violence, after all. Whatever faults he had—and she conceded he had a few—were balanced by her own eagerness to run risks. It was the only way she knew how to live, or cared to. The space between someone's arms was still the most mysterious of the world's great uncharted regions and definitely not for the fainthearted.

"Hello, Johnny," she said, wishing they could exchange nicknames and slaps on the back like in the old carefree days. But she was still the focus of everyone's attention and merely said, still at a respectable distance, "I understand you're in Rock and Roll." She put heavy emphasis on each word. "I see your name quite often," she said.

"You put on a great show out there," he said.

"You saw it?"

"You were terrific," he lied. He'd been across town.

"Really?"

"The best I ever saw. Congratulations."

"You're no slouch yourself."

"Yeah, but you—just look at you."

"What's wrong with the way I look?"

"You look terrific. Did you get the roses?"

221

"Which roses?"

"Never mind. The phone works both ways, you know—I'm in the book."

"Well, I was meaning to call, but—"

There was no titillation, no choice dialogue. He split his sides once or twice, ran out of cigarettes and borrowed one from somebody. His tongue was in shape, but after a few minutes of watching him, she began to wonder why he had come. He wasn't the old Johnny she remembered. In fact, she didn't know him at all.

"You haven't changed," he said to her.

"There are just twelve notes," she said.

"I'm making a fortune with less," he boasted.

"I'm not doing too badly, either," she said.

Then he came to the point. "Yeah, but you could be doing better."

"How's that?" she wanted to know.

"Your royalties. I know what your setup is," he said, suddenly all serious. "Your contract's up with Decca next month. I wish you'd think of me—" She was flabbergasted. "We're a small label, but not for long. I don't care what they offer you, no matter what the deal is, I'll beat it. I'd like for us to get back together."

She was getting sick—sick of climbers like him who had run up her back pell-mell ever since she could remember, sick of his smoke that was all that ever came out of his mouth, sick of all the killers in this world who lay in wait to exploit mothers and small children, sick of that asinine look on his face. What a monster he truly was. He didn't love his own child, had never made an effort to see either of them until today, and now this. So now he wanted the two of them, or the three of them, to get back together. What rank hypocrisy—what a smirk, moreover.

"So whadda you think?" he asked her.

"That's the only reason you came, isn't it?" she said, controlling admirably the tremolo in her voice.

"What?"

"That's the only reason you came here tonight was to ask me whether I—"

"No, I can explain. Wait a minute, Francine."

"Call my agent," she said.

She rejoined the others and left him standing there, the entire incident creating scarcely a ripple. The other guests were not aware of what had been said and didn't know who Boyle was. His face had never been on any magazines, and they had hardly come to see him anyway. They clustered around her, their wings fluttering, alighting on her shoulders or in the gentleness of her hand. A star must wear her armor and mustn't break, but when she saw him move toward the door, she had to speak. She couldn't let him go like that without saying something for posterity. Famous last words, so to speak, like Pocahontas and John Smith. So she called to him and said the first thing that entered her mind. "Johnny, do you think Rock and Roll is here to stay?" she said.

He turned in the doorway. He couldn't tell if she was joking, but she must be. "Do I think Rock and Roll is here to stay?" he said.

"Rock and Roll?" some of the guests tittered. It was well known to be nothing but a current fad propagated by juvenile delinquents, on the order of stink bombs.

"Yes," he said.

They laughed and turned back to Francine, only to discover that she had summarily disappeared into the bedroom. She was not to come out again for the longest time. As they waited for her, some said that she had been crying as she locked herself in, while others said that wasn't so—they tended to blame her actions on female troubles. Or maybe she didn't like Rock and Roll. But there *was* that strange man, ominous-looking even as he smiled, still standing there.

Afterwards, after all the extras had gone home and the sound technicians were out of sight, they walked alone. OVERHEAD CRANE SHOT, BLIMP SHOT, TRACKING SHOT, JUMP SHOT. It was a street at the back of Metro-Goldwyn-Mayer, and raindrops had started to fall. Since it was Southern California, neither of them had an umbrella. She was off to London the next day, and he was off to South Philly to ink a new singer named Bobby. They held hands. There was only to-night, and that's the way it should have been from the very beginning. A short walk instead of a long shot. They both knew that now.

LONG SHOT, LOVE THEME COMES UP, REVERSE-ANGLE SHOT, WIDE-ANGLE SHOT, CAMERA TRACKS R–L and PANS L–R, DOLLY SHOT, OVERHEAD CRANE SHOT, BLIMP SHOT . . . HOLD ON young lovers in a world of their own. SLOW FADE AND BRING MUSIC UP, and that should do it nicely. Keep it simple and poignant. Lights.